ASHLEY MACK

The Scent of You

CONTENT WARNING: sibling abuse, kidnapping, fire and injuries from fire, graphic sex and sexual situations including spitting, spanking, restraints, and dirty talk; death, murder, and mayhem.

First edition

ISBN: 978-1-960161-06-2

Cover art by Rachel McEwan

This book was professionally typeset on Reedsy.
Find out more at reedsy.com

To my puppy, Whiskey.

"There is no "should" or "should not" when it comes to having feelings. They're part of who we are and and their origins are beyond our control."

- FRED ROGERS

Contents

Where Were We...   iii

1   Gailen   1

2   Aspen   6

3   Aspen   9

4   Gailen   13

5   Gailen   17

6   Aspen   22

7   Gailen   27

8   Gailen   33

9   Aspen   39

10   Gailen   43

11   Aspen   45

12   Gailen   50

13   Aspen   57

14   Gailen   61

15   Aspen   64

16   Gailen   70

17   Aspen   76

18   Aspen   81

19   Gailen   87

20   Aspen   94

21   Gailen   102

22   Gailen   106

23   Aspen   110

24 Aspen   113

25 Gailen   119

26 Aspen   127

27 Gailen   133

28 Aspen   140

29 Gailen   148

30 Aspen   153

31 Gailen   157

32 Aspen   162

33 Gailen   168

34 Aspen   174

35 Gailen   180

36 Gailen   186

37 Aspen   190

38 Gailen   199

39 Aspen   205

40 Gailen   208

41 Aspen   212

42 Aspen   215

43 Gailen   221

44 Epilogue - Gailen   227

45 Epilogue - Aspen   232

Playlist   237

Acknowledgments   238

Also by Ashley Mack   239

About the Author   240

Where Were We…

It's been four years.

The four original Sorrelle sisters met their soulmates, had families, grieved their past and tried to build their futures.

But something was missing.

We left with Gailen recovering from his injuries and agreeing to hunt the surprise fifth sister - Aspen Forrester. After four long years, he's tracked down her location.

He's going to be very surprised by what he finds.

This is the end of the story.

Note: Aspen was horribly abused by her brother, and recognized her trauma once she got away. This is not the story of how she healed, but know that she did and engaged with professionals for help. This is the story of the last pieces being resolved to allow her to move on, but true recovery is a journey that never ends.

1

Gailen

The nightmare never starts with fire, it starts with darkness. A dim, unfamiliar hallway the takes me further away from the flames, even as the sound of the crackling burn gets louder as it devours more of the house.

I find her in the room at the end of the hall. There's nothing in it, not even a mattress, and despite the cool temperature she's in only shorts and a t-shirt. Bruises cover her legs, and her left knee is swollen and a dark, mottled purple. Like someone stomped on it in an effort to get her to stop moving.

The girl, Aspen, is curled up in a ball with her arms around her head.

I move toward her, already reaching to pick her up when she lifts her head and her steely, dark gaze meets mine. I've never seen anyone so hopeless, and I've seen a lot of hopeless things in my life. She's not afraid of me, but she moves away. As if she could disappear into the wall.

"Come with me, I've got you. Your sisters are waiting for you."

"No. Go. Leave me here. Please, please leave me here."

"You'll burn!" The crackling fire is getting louder, and I know that we are running out of time. If I have to fight her to get her out of here,

I will. I don't want to knock her out but if I have to do that, I will.

"Then let me burn!" Her voice is raw and raspy. "Please!"

Aspen is begging me to let her die.

In the dream, I stand there in the room until the fire consumes us both. The flames lick along my body and I listen to her scream. The burning gives way to numbness as it eats my nerves, but the feeling of failure never decreases. It pounds against me in waves as the screams go on and on.

In reality, I ran deeper into the room and picked her up. Her knee was so jacked she couldn't run away if she tried.

"Do you want me to die?" I asked her.

"No." She whimpered, and it was enough. If she couldn't live for herself, in that moment she was living for me. I ran out into the hallway and saw nothing but flames at the end of it. None of the other doors in the hall would open, so into the blaze I went. There was a clear path from the hall to the door outside as long as I could move fast enough. I pulled Aspen tight against me and ran.

At some point something dropped onto my back, and the pain was like nothing I'd ever experienced before. I remember seeing the Sorrelles, then the sky, and then nothing. I remember telling myself that I couldn't let Aspen go until I knew she was safe.

When I wake up from the nightmare, I always replay the real ending in my head. That I got Aspen out. That she had a few burns but was otherwise unharmed. Even her knee healed. I saved her, and it cost me, but I would do it again. She needed me. From everything I learned about her while I healed, she had needed someone to believe that she was worth the risk of saving.

After I healed from my burns, a long and excruciating process, I started looking for her.

I needed a purpose, and that's what Aspen became. We understood something inside each other.

The look in her eyes was the only explanation I needed for why she ran in the first place. If I had been that hopeless, I don't think I could have stayed either. For everyone else, it was a happy moment. Lovers reuniting, a family becoming whole, a time for celebration.

For Aspen, it was freedom from her chains, but she saw it as a new set of obligations and expectations. Another time when her choices were being taken away, and everyone thought they new better than her. Aspen was shattered in a way they couldn't understand. Even I don't, but I could see it when they wouldn't.

Although I would say Aspen isn't totally broken, or at the very least being on her own has been healing for her. In the last four years of looking for her, she's displayed plenty of sass, humor, and personality. It reminds me of her sisters, and I feel both gratitude and guilt with every reminder.

I failed the Sorrelles. It was my job to protect Don, and I was more worried about following his instructions and making him feel better when he was having a difficult time than I was about his immediate safety. I left the house, the assassin came in, and I lost him. I'll never understand why the Sorrelles didn't kill me. Why they weren't angrier with me for failing them all.

Anora and Owen told me plenty of times that they didn't blame me, and if I'd been there I would have only ended up dead on the library floor. I'm not sure if I believe that, but I appreciate their sentiment. Even Aro has forgiven me, and she's the one that took everything the hardest.

It doesn't matter what they say. A debt is owed. I will never stop until I bring Aspen home.

I get up from my current hotel bed and stretch, then walk over to the messenger bag that's accompanied me on years worth of searching for the surprise Sorrelle sister. Inside is a file of every location I've ever tracked her to, usually too late, and a small stack of various pieces of paper.

Hi Gailen, I left some brownies in the kitchen for you.

That one was from the first time I had a location to track and found she'd been at a small farmhouse in rural Pennsylvania. Almost a year after she fled from the hospital.

Happy Birthday Gailen!

That was her apartment in St. Louis. She'd also left me a key chain that said "Meet Me in St. Louis" with the Arch on it. A cheeky present, but if I pulled out my keys now, the plastic piece would be there.

Merry Christmas G-Bear! I'm sorry to say you're on the naughty list. Better luck next year!

And there was a small pile of charcoal next to the note. That was in the tiny place she'd rented out in the New Mexico desert. It was the closest I'd come to catching her. There had only been hours between her leaving and me finding the place and I was sure of that because she'd left a lot of things behind. I packed it all up, put it in my SUV, and got back to the search.

There was always a theme based on the location or time, and I learned more about her than I think she realized with those notes. Her humor, her inexperience, the way that she was exploring and engaging with the world because she'd never had a chance to before. I got to see Aspen grow. I got to experience her in a way that even though I could have, I never shared with her family. Those notes were between the two of us.

The last note, from a little rental on the water in Florida, was from over 2 months ago.

G-Money, I promise I'm okay. Go have a life. Love, Aspen.

It was a different tone than anything she'd left me before, and it made me worried. It could mean that things were turning around for her, or it could mean that she was giving up. My biggest fear was that I would come to one of these places and find her body. That Aspen would give up before I could find her and put some hope back into her eyes.

Before I could explain to her that she had a place to belong.

Four long years, but I would never give up.

I'd tracked her to North Dakota. I knew she was already gone, but today I'd look through the apartment she abandoned for any evidence of where she'd been and where she might go. As the years went on, she only got better at hiding, but her confidence could also be her undoing. I was counting on it.

There's a note on the kitchen counter in the apartment, with a menu for a restaurant.

You look sad lately, want to taco bout it? Find me and we'll chat. Love, Aspen

2

Aspen

What I'm doing is mean. Meaner than they can imagine.

Because I haven't been on the run. I've been playing misdirection.

After my friend Monty got me my new identity - hi, I'm Aspen Peat - and I got every liquid cent I could get my hands on, I disappeared into the emptiness of Wyoming. No one noticed a teenager living by herself. As long as I didn't make trouble, they never asked questions. I bought a perfect little A-frame, put in the best technology, and started working freelance in addition to my work with my hacker collective.

When I got bored, I'd leave for a few weeks to lay a trail for Gailen to follow, hang out until he was on his way, and then I'd leave him a note so he knew I was fine. If it was anyone other than him that was looking for me, I think I would have let the trail go cold. But Gailen was good and he cared, and I wanted him to feel like he had a purpose after I nearly got him killed.

I owe him. Sometimes I hate him, sometimes I want to relive that night and change what happened, but nothing changes that I am indebted to him for my life. It took a lot of therapy for me to get to that point, and I think messing with him helps me forgive him.

Right now, he's wandering around the little apartment I rented in

Fargo, looking through the things I acquired and then abandoned. He looks good. It's been a few months since I've seen him, and I'm always watching for signs that he's in pain. The first few times were awful. The way he moved was stiff and intentional, as if one wrong move would break him. I'd been tracking his healing and knew he was doing well but I can't imagine what it was like for him.

Other than the slight twisting of my eyelid and the scarring on my arm, it's not obvious at all that he saved me from a fire. No one would even know I'd ever been in that kind of danger at all.

A lot's happened in 4 years. Most of it good. I got to eat whatever and whenever I wanted. I hiked national parks, I learned how to swim, and I started rock climbing. I grew 6 inches and gained 50 pounds. It was incredible. The freedom was dangerously intoxicating, but I also never lost my sense of fear.

The fear of being seen. The fear of being trapped. The fear of someone thinking that they had any right to control my actions or tell me what to do with my time, space, appetite, or body. I was better off alone because then I never had to be afraid of lashing out at someone who didn't deserve it, and I never had to explain myself.

I eat popcorn while I watch him look through the clothes I left in the closet.

My dog, Troy, puts his head on my knee and watches the screen with me. I wonder if he would know Gailen on sight from how many times we've done this exact same thing. Watching the man on the screen look frustrated or defeated, but always amused. He always smirks at the notes. He can't help himself.

I think that's why I keep leaving them. I like that he smiles for me.

I stayed on the down low for awhile. I told myself I was going to stop leaving crumbs. I was going to let them all go. I wanted them to move on the way they deserved. Even though I knew that my sisters had moved forward, I also knew how invested they still were in finding me. I didn't want that for them.

The only thing I was to them was a symbol of a painful past that they deserved to close the door on. I knew I'd be welcome back, but there was a reason I didn't go. Even if I was tired of being alone, of running, or of looking over my shoulder, I wouldn't bring my chaos into their life.

Their whole lives they'd been a foursome, and I didn't want to upset that dynamic.

I'd been alone for my first 15 years, I was still fine alone at 19, and I'd be fine alone for the rest of my life.

I had Troy. I was fine.

Gailen picked up the note on the table and read it again.

He smiled. I smiled. I closed the window on the cameras, and went back to work.

3

Aspen

Troy and I are wandering over our land like we usually do. Sometimes, when I look out across the fields and up into the impossible sky, I don't feel lonely. I feel small, but I'm okay with that. I'm okay knowing that I am the center of my own universe, and likely irrelevant to the rest of the world.

I close my eyes and imagine myself as dust on the wind, floating through the air, touching things for a moment before moving on.

Troy runs around and then circles back to me, checking that I'm okay. He does this over and over. I rely on him as much as he relies on me. A dog is the perfect partner when you want to care for something without heavy expectations. I meet his basic needs, and he adds to my happiness. I take a deep breath and listen for him as he runs and enjoys his life.

A sharp cry pulls me out of my meditative state.

I run to Troy and can already tell he's hurt. His front paw is pulled up and in to his body, and there's blood standing out on the white fur of his paws. He's a mutt that's mostly a fluffy brown but he's got white socks. My stomach drops with fear. He's all I have. I need Troy to be okay.

I don't know what he stepped on, but it cut him open and it went in deep. Luckily, it doesn't appear that there's anything embedded in his paw.

The good thing is that we aren't far from the house so I can lift him easily and carry him back. I clean up the wound, but it's still bleeding. Fear makes me sweat, and I load Troy into the back of my Land Rover and give him a treat so he'll stay laying down. Generally, he's well-trained and does what I say. He gives a pathetic lick of my hand when I wrap a blanket around him.

There's an emergency vet in town and they should still be open by the time I get there, which is nearly 45 minutes of driving. The sun is just starting to fade as I pull into the main streets and past the usual businesses. I'm sure most of the vet's emergency business is farm animals, but if I can't be frivolous about my dog, then what's the point?

I pull up to the small white house that serves as the vet practice, and leave Troy inside the car as I go in to see if they have time to see him.

"Hey honey, what's going on?" A pleasant nurse asks me, her brown hair fading to gray.

"My dog hurt his paw and it looks pretty deep."

"We got time, bring him in. Dr. Murray will take a look."

I nod and thank her, and then go back outside to get Troy. I carry him inside and then set him down gently. He still keeps his paw up, but sits to give his body a rest. The nurse comes around the counter and greets him, letting him smell her hand before she gives him a gentle pat. He wags his tail but it's subdued.

I rub Troy's head to relax us both as she gets information from me.

An older man who looks kind of like Santa comes out from the back. He's even got little gold framed glasses and looks over the rim to meet my eyes. For a moment he gets a strange look on his face, like he's trying to figure something out about me. I don't like it.

"Troy?" he says in a soft grumble.

Troy stands at attention and moves toward the vet. If Troy had gotten bad vibes, we'd be out of there, but he has no problem with Dr. Murray, so we both follow him into an exam room. I get Troy up on the table and Dr. Murray examines him generally before looking at the wounded paw.

"Nice, healthy dog. Good coat."

Troy whimpers when he prods the wound.

"Alright, missy, we got something stuck deep in there, must've broken off when he was running. I'm going to have to do a local anesthetic, remove the object, then we'll seal it up and probably give you some antibiotics to prevent infection. Sound good?"

"Yes, thank you so much."

"You ever live in Chicago?" he asks.

I flinch and hope he didn't see it. "Nope. Born and raised out here."

"I feel like I've seen you before."

"Maybe I just have one of those faces." I force a smile. No one who says that has one of those faces. The people who have those faces are generally unmemorable for a reason.

"I moved out here from the city a few years back. I'd swear I saw you. Any family back there?"

"No, sir."

Dr. Murray focuses his gaze on me and there's nothing I can do except stand there and let him analyze my face. I try to keep my expression pleasant but blank.

"Funny," he finally says. He steps out to get the nurse, and they get everything ready while I pet Troy and seek comfort from him. As they start to work, I rub his cheeks and ears and try to get him to keep his focus on me. Other than a few whimpers, he's very well-behaved and they get the removal done quickly.

There's an ugly, bloody splinter of wood, like maybe the tip of a stick stabbed him and broke off inside his paw. My stomach turns with nausea, and I bury my face in Troy's warm neck. He licks my ear and I smile at him. Such a good dog.

They wrap up the wound, and Dr. Murray steps out as the nurse explains the necessary after care to me, as well as when, and some advice on how, to get Troy to take his antibiotics. Honestly, any people food and Troy won't care that there are pills in it.

Dr. Murray is at the desk as we slowly walk to the door of the office. "You be safe now," he tells me. "I'll figure out where I know you from!" I'm sure he's teasing, but the possibility stops me cold. There's no way he knows me, and even if he knows the Sorrelles, there's no way for him to connect them to me. It's not like they've publicly been talking about their secret sister.

He won't figure out who I am, and it hasn't compromised anything. I repeat that in my head over and over as we get to the Land Rover. Logically, I know this, but it doesn't make the fear that this is all going to come to an end any less real.

I let Troy ride in the front seat and try to convince myself there's nothing to worry about as I drive back to our home in the one of a kind dark of rural Wyoming.

Maybe it's time I was found. Maybe my luck is running out. I have Troy and it helps to have him, but I am lonely sometimes. I am tired of doing everything all by myself. If I get caught, I get caught. I'm done fighting.

That's the truth, I realize as I climb into bed.

The apartment in Fargo was my last crumb. Not because I'm hiding, but because I don't care that he's looking anymore. If Gailen finds me, I'll cooperate.

Mostly.

4

Gailen

My phone rings and I don't recognize the number, so I let it go to voicemail. I look up the area code and see that it's Wyoming. I don't know anybody out there, so I can probably safely assume that it's a spam call.

After the apartment in Fargo, I didn't have anywhere else to go, so I hung around for awhile. Had a few beers, ate some really good tacos at Aspen's sarcastic recommendation, and enjoyed a small break from my life on the hunt for Aspen Sorrelle. I didn't know where to go next, and this was as good of a place as any to regroup before heading back to Chicago.

Currently, I'm in a sports bar pretending to watch a game I don't care about, and pretending like I remember how to be social. My phone buzzes on the bar top and whoever called left a voicemail.

I open it up and let it play, reading the transcript faster than the voice talks.

"Mr. Burke you probably don't remember me but my name is Alvin Murray, I used to be a veterinarian in Chicago who did some volunteer work for the Sorrelles. That girl y'all were keeping an eye out for? I saw her. She's here." He names a town and I'm assuming it's in Wyoming since that's where he's calling me from. It's also concerning that when he says "volunteer work," he means that he would come play doctor when something happened that couldn't involve hospitals. He plays both sides of the law.

That's not someone I can trust easily, and I definitely don't want to trust him with Aspen. Especially when, if memory serves, we told him very clearly about the reward should he assist in finding her. It's $1.2 million. That's nothing to sneeze at or lie about.

I throw some cash on the bar for a beer I didn't touch, and step outside.

"Dr. Murray." He answers after only one ring.

"Gailen Burke. Tell me what you saw."

Dr. Murray describes Aspen to me, that he saw her dog for an injury, and that based on her paperwork he has an address. That's more direct information than I've ever had before. For the first time in four years, Aspen wasn't careful. She maybe even made a mistake.

"I'm on my way to you now. If I confirm that it's her, the money is yours."

"Well now, I think a little good faith needs to be offered. You're not the only ones looking for her." He sounds smug and I don't like it.

I stop in my tracks, almost to my hotel. "What are you talking about?"

"A year or so back, someone else circulated her picture too. They offered a reward for information, period, not only if she was found."

I sigh and pinch the bridge of my nose. "What do you want?"

"$50,000 to start. The rest if it's her."

I have enough money in the discretionary accounts the Sorrelles have setup for my search to pay that easily, but something about this feels exceptionally slimy. It's also the best lead I've had in a long time that I don't suspect was dropped by Aspen herself. This might be my first and only chance to catch her off guard.

"Done. The money will be transferred when I get to you, and you

14

give me what you have."

It only takes a few hours for me to get everything together and get on a plane. I fly into Casper, pick up my rental and a few other supplies, and I start making the drive to the small town where the vet now lives. The small town that might belong to Aspen at the moment. Mostly she's hid herself in big cities where she isn't noticed easily. Living in a place like this, even in keep-your-business-to-yourself Wyoming, is a risk.

A risk that might be working in my favor right now, since she did get noticed.

It also means that she has a pet of some kind, or there would be no reason for her to have gone to the vet. She never had a pet with her, or at least no signs of one, at any of the locations I tracked her. Something about all of this feels weird, but I go with it.

I hit the vet's office first thing the next morning.

It's a small, cozy building and it smells like animals. In a good way. In that walking the line between comforting and unpleasant wet fur smell.

A smiling woman greets me, but something about my expression takes her back. It feels off, somehow. I believe that Aspen is here, but my instincts are catching flags all over the place although I can't articulate what's setting me off.

We didn't know someone else was looking for Aspen.

That's terrifying, frankly. It makes every move I make more urgent because I don't trust this vet, and if she really is here, Aspen has no idea that her information is compromised.

"Dr. Murray said he needed to see me," I tell her. She gives me a tight smile and steps into the back. After a few moments, the man himself comes to the front and gestures me to the back of the building.

Once we're in his office, he closes the door and then hands me a piece of paper from his desk. It's got a name, Aspen Peat, as well as an

15

address, phone number, and some other information in addition to details about her dog, Troy.

I pull out my phone and login to my banking app.

"Ready when you are," I tell Dr. Murray. "If it's her, you'll have the rest by the end of the week."

The man grins and it feels gross, but I follow his instructions to send the money to his account. Dr. Murray stares at his computer screen, clicking refresh over and over, until the transaction goes through.

"We're all clear," he tells me.

"You share this information with anyone else, and you won't live long enough to spend a dime."

He pales underneath his beard when I wait until he looks away from his account and into my eyes. He needs to know that I'm serious.

"They'll never find you."

After a long moment in which he swallows harshly, Dr. Murray nods.

I give him a nod in return and leave the office. When I get back to the lobby I try to give a less grumpy look to the nurse but she's distracted by the computer. This is a solid lead, and now it's time to track Aspen when she doesn't know I'm coming.

And hopefully before anyone else knows she's here.

5

Gailen

First, I drive to the address on the form. It's isolated but surrounded by open spaces so there's not a lot of options to hide. I note a green Land Rover in the driveway, and write down the license plate number to track down later.

I drive back toward town until I find somewhere to stop and pull off to waste some time, where a random car on the side of the road won't be something of note. Then I wait. Either until dark when I can approach the cabin, or until she leaves it so I can follow her.

A few hours into my vigil, the Land Rover drives by. I confirm that it's the same by the plates since it's not exactly a rare vehicle out here. After letting her get a bit ahead, I follow her into town.

Aspen isn't expecting this, so she's not as careful. She's not paying attention to the cars around her and if they're following the same route. Even from cars back I can see her moving her head and singing along with whatever she's listening to and it makes me smile a little. It's so normal.

I park outside the grocery store and watch her go inside. It's the first time I've fully seen her, in person, since I pulled her out of the burning house.

She's tall but on the slim side, wearing worn-in baggy jeans and a hoodie that's way too big for her. Her hair is pulled up in a ponytail and stuck through the hole of a snapback hat. It's the same rich brown as her sisters, and she has their olive skin as well. There's no doubt, even from a distance, that she's a Sorrelle.

There's no doubt in my mind that it's her when she walks out of the store with bags of groceries and I see her from the front. She's got piercing dark eyes, and a face that's a mix of Aster and Anora - soft mouth, sharp, dark eyes, and a rounded nose. The look on her face though, that's all Aspen. Guarded but trying to force neutrality.

Everything with her is a mask, and not everyone can see that it's there.

I've been studying the changes in her for the past four years. There's nothing about her that I can't see. Parts of her are a mystery to me, but I know how she thinks. Protecting herself is her first priority. Being nothing to anyone is all that she wants.

Like it or not, she'll always be something to me.

After she puts her bags in the trunk she stops and looks around slowly. I wouldn't doubt that she can feel my eyes on her, but even as hers move over my truck they don't linger. Aspen feels something but she can't figure out what it is, or realize that it's me. Or maybe she does, but it's too new for her to follow that feeling to find me.

I follow her back to her house, and when she's safely inside I start checking the perimeter. There are no proximity sensors or invisible fencing, but there are cameras. The lack of paranoia is surprising. Aspen must feel extremely secure here.

Looking through the windows, I see her cooking, and I get a glimpse of her dog. He's brown with white paws and looks at her with pure love in his eyes. She looks back with the same, and I feel an odd loosening in my chest to know that she has something, anything, that makes her happy. I was afraid that Aspen was so isolated that she'd still be the broken girl I dragged out of a burning house.

I can see so easily that she's more.

I wish telling the Sorrelles that would be enough, but I know better.

Aspen looks up and out the window, exactly where I'm hiding. If I didn't know better, I'd think we were making eye contact right now. Her face stills, and I see her more clearly now. She's still obviously young but I can see the age inside her after everything she's been through. Aspen is tough, self-sufficient, and behind walls so high and so thick it would take years to break through them.

She's also beautiful.

So beautiful it makes my chest hurt and my heart ache.

No one that beautiful should be that sad.

I retreat back to where I've hidden my truck and get some sleep.

The next day, I wait some more, and get rewarded with Aspen's Land Rover leaving her house. Exactly what I needed, although I don't know how much time I'll have. It all depends on her errand.

The door to Aspen's house is locked, but it's not hard to pick. It wasn't hard to avoid the cameras either, and I make a note of her blind spots. She has a security system, but it's one I know, so I type in the override command that turns it off. The dog, Troy, must be with her because the kennel in the dining room is empty.

The A-frame is plain but nice. It's got a large open living space, dining area, and kitchen. In front of me is a staircase to a loft where Aspen sleeps, and to the left are doors that lead to another bedroom and a bathroom.

Looking around, I'm struck by all of the details that cover the space. There are framed posters of old movies on the walls, shelves with books and nick-knacks - mostly brain toys like a Rubik's cube and various wooden puzzle boxes. In the kitchen there are appliances and other convenience items, and the cabinets are full of dishes and silverware.

It's lived in, and not new.

Inside the bedroom in the loft, there's a closet and dresser full of clothes. A picture of her mother on the nightstand. Laundry in a pile in a hamper. A TV and a cabinet full of DVDs. The room smells like citrus and and sandalwood, and I catch myself before I lean over and inhale her bed sheets.

The feeling in the pit of my stomach deepens when I go to the downstairs bedroom.

There's a futon, but the rest of the space is dominated by desks and computers, multiple towers and monitors, and the constant low buzz of machines that are always running.

Aspen didn't just throw this place together. She didn't end up here after running from Fargo.

She *lives* here. She's been living here for a long time. This is a settled home. A place that's clearly lived in and loved, and has collected the layers of belongings and signs of long ownership. This is a safe place to her and it is not new in any way. The story of the last four years of her life is all over this place, and it's a treasure trove for someone who has only gotten bits and pieces.

Knowing that she's been healthy and taking care of herself is a relief. Aspen was always safe. There was never the uncertainty I feared.

It won't stop me from telling her sisters that I've found her, and probably shattering the safety of this place for her. Especially now that I know someone else has been looking for her. It's more important than ever to get her connected with her family, and to find a way to keep her safe from there.

Aspen might want to be isolated, but she needs to learn that doesn't mean she has to be alone.

I'm kind of pissed off this means that every place I've chased her in the last four years has been nothing but a tease. She'd pick a random place, far away from this home base of hers, drop enough of a hint to make me come running, and then dip out. It would be infuriating if it wasn't also kind of impressive. I'm weirdly proud of her for keeping herself safe and steady for so long. By the trails she left for me over and over, and how damn creative she had to be to do do that.

Aspen is a wonder. We really had been playing a game for years.

But I have a feeling that wasn't going to last, even if I wasn't the one to find her. There's a stirring in my gut, and I always trust my instincts. Something is coming, and it's going to get ugly. She's hid too well for too long, and so few good things last.

I slip outside and hide in the yard, waiting for my prey to return.

6

Aspen

I came back from Troy's check-up and I knew something was different. Someone had been here.

Nothing was moved, but the air was different. The sandalwood scent was similar to what I wore and used, but there was something smoky too. I walked through the house and Troy bounded after me. I watched him to see if he noticed anything or smelled anything in particular, but Troy was his usual self.

In my bedroom, the smell was stronger, like whoever had been here lingered there.

Heat bloomed in my core, and that was an unfamiliar feeling.

The feeling that I was being watched had floated in and out of my mind for the last few days, and now I believed it. Someone was watching me. Someone had been interested enough to follow me and come inside my house.

There's only one person who would do that.

Gailen.

Maybe Gailen had found me.

The idea should have filled me with dread, but it also made me kind of excited. This was a change in our game and I wanted to see what he would do. I had no doubt that when I was ready I could run again without him stopping me. As tired as I was, I still deserved to be alone. I still deserved to pay for what I had done and been part of because of Elton.

This was the life I would lead until I died.

I had promised myself that.

But it didn't mean I couldn't make things interesting every once and awhile.

So game on, Gailen. I'm waiting for you.

I wake up slowly, but I know I'm not alone.

Troy is awake at the end of the bed, tail wagging softly, but head still down as if he woke up and saw someone he knew. It's odd to me that whoever it is, if it is Gailen, has so easily earned the trust of my dog. Troy is well-behaved but he gets excited about new people and wants to explore them. The fact that he hasn't moved to seek this person out is odd.

"I know you're here, Gailen." I take a chance and speak my guess into the darkness. I'm not sure if I'm expecting a response or not. After a few minutes of silence pass, I keep going. There's a pressure inside my chest like I have a lot to say to him, and this might be my only chance.

"I know I sent you on a wild goose chase, but I wanted them to know I was okay without getting too close. I can't..." I swallow hard around the sudden lump in my throat. "Even here, sometimes I feel the need to run, and I run somewhere you can find me. I know Elton is dead but...I can't escape my own mind. I can't escape remembering him and how he controlled my entire life for so long. So I run."

More silence. I can't even hear breathing. The scent of sandalwood again feels deeper, stronger, because it's coming from two of us now. I like the idea that we like the same scents, and smell so similar. I want to know why he also smells like smoke. Not like cigarettes, but like campfire, or the first burning of the leaves in the fall. A smell I didn't even know existed until after I started my new life.

Even if I'm talking to no one in the dark, it feels good to get it off my chest.

"I'm happy here, but I never feel safe. I don't think I ever will. There's no such thing as true safety, you know? It's like the idea that we can die at any time, that's why we're never safe. There's always something to be on guard against. Something to wait for. Some hit or pain or loss. I'm so tired." My head crashes to my chest and I fight the tears again.

Elton would hurt me when I cried, so at a young age I got very good at holding my tears in, or getting rid of the need to cry at all. Once he was gone, I felt a lot more freedom. I laughed, I cried, every emotion felt more intense and the need to express them in the most intense way broke through too.

It meant even when I safely made my way here, I still made some questionable and destructive decisions. Like stealing cars and breaking into properties so I could hide until I got my new identity.

Driving across the country and hopping from hacker friend to hacker friend, finally meeting them in person. It was was fun but questionable. I smoked weed for the first time with Si and then stayed high for days because I liked feeling so damn relaxed.

I lost my virginity to Tuck and we fucked like dumb horny rabbits for a week straight and then I left, and have refused to speak to him about anything except jobs since. We were each other's first and I think it hurt us both in the end, but felt really good at the time.

I went to a giant amusement park and I rode the same roller coasters over and over until I got physically sick, puking up my cotton candy into a trash can.

I bought a gun and learned to shoot, and sometimes I lock Troy up and go shoot at targets for fun, for the release, for the certainty of the knowledge that I still know how and I'm still a good shot, and that I could kill someone if they threatened me.

"I know you want to take me to them, but I'm going to ask that you don't. I'm not ready and I don't know if I ever will be. I don't want to break things any further than they've already been broken."

Troy's tail thumps harder, and I pat the bed so he moves up by me. He rests his head on my upper thigh and looks up at me with love.

"I dream about you," my voice is so soft I wonder if he'll hear me. "I dream about you saving me and it's not a nightmare. In the dream I feel you come into the room before I see you, and I know that even though I'm afraid, I can go with you. Sometimes it's just you carrying me somewhere, my arms around your neck, and I know that I'm okay." I sigh again. "I trust you in the dream, Gailen. For some reason, I trust you now. I need you to trust me back and let me go."

Tears stream down my cheeks and I think about the things I usually shut out. I think about the few days I got with my sisters, when they never for a second shut me out or shut me down, and they welcomed me into their circle like the space had only been waiting for me to fill it. Aro's laugh when she was winning at a game. Anora's hugs whenever she thought I needed it. Aster narrowing her eyes when she asked me questions about my hacks and digital attacks. Alina calling me "Auntie Aspen" with no hesitation or doubt in her voice and showing me little Wyn. Even Harp, Owen, and Isaac endeared themselves to me. Harp thinking he had a good poker face, and Isaac setting up games on my phone so I wouldn't get bored. Owen's steady presence and understanding about what my life had been like.

How could I care about people so much that I'd only known in person for days? I didn't want to care about them.

Maybe because I'd known them virtually for most of my life. Elton made me watch them, made me think they were my family but that they didn't want me, and I learned everything about them. It only took days to undo his damage when it came to them because the second I was in their presence, the lie was so obvious.

And I had hurt them. These people I loved, who had no reason to love me, had been hurt over and over because of me.

"Let me go," I said again, into the dark. When no answer came, I rolled over and snuggled down next to Troy and cried until I fell asleep.

7

Gailen

I listened to Aspen talk into the dark and nearly lost control. The desire to go to her, hold her, convince her that she was safe, was more than I'd ever felt before in my life. I wanted to take her in my arms and tell her she was safe with *me*. That I would make her safe.

That was completely irrational.

Something felt different inside me when I was in her presence. It was inexplicable and inconvenient.

I kept telling myself that she was a 19 year old kid, but I knew that was a lie. She might be young, but Aspen had been forced to age beyond her years. I don't think she'd ever had a chance to be a kid, and she made herself become a successful and amazing adult. All I wanted was for her to not only *be* safe, but feel safe. I didn't know how I could give it to her, but I knew that I would try.

I'd been standing outside her bedroom door, hidden in the dark of the hallway. I could see her clearly but she couldn't see me. She'd been wearing a tank top and nothing underneath it, and I noticed her body in a way that I couldn't help. The tight lines of her muscular arms, the elegant curve of her long neck, the small swells of her breasts and the obvious sight of her nipples, hard beneath the cotton Aspen was the most perfect woman I had ever seen.

I never reacted like this when I saw her on video or in photos. It was something about her physical presence that awoke a ferocious demand in me that I didn't understand. Or want.

When I was sure she was asleep again, I left the house. I got back to my truck, drove to the airport, and got on a plane to Chicago. I hadn't really slept in days, I definitely hadn't showered, and I was a disaster of unkempt hair and five o'clock shadow.

Showing up looking like this was unprofessional, but I think me and the Sorrelle family were past the demand for professionalism at this point. I'd never stop feeling guilty, but I also knew that I was doing this to myself more than they were. Owen let me run after Aspen because he knew I needed it, and the family wanted it done. Despite my failure, they trusted me with this important task.

The guards at the house didn't know me, and even though they let me inside they had their hands on their guns. I pulled up short when I saw that everyone was there. All of the sisters, their men, their kids - the people that I knew existed but barely saw. There was really only one person I wanted to tell this to, and after a minute she came out of the library.

They must have started using that room again.

"I found her," I said to Anora, and felt a sense of relief at her delighted shock.

Anora looked at Owen. "Dining room."

He nodded and walked off, calling out as he went. Aster, Alina, and Aro came out behind Anora and they all had a similar shocked look. I think after so long not finding her they must have felt in the back of their minds that we never would. I never would. This was closure they deserved, and probably needed.

A door into a piece of Don's life that had been separate from them. A blunt reminder that their father was a man, and human. I hoped

Aspen would give them a chance.

Anora was a little dazed, so Alina stepped up and moved everyone toward the dining room. They all took seats and I stood at the far end of the table. Even though they'd invited me to plenty of meals, I never sat. I know they cared about their staff and they paid us well, but we weren't them. We weren't the family, and that line would always be there. I didn't sit at the table, period.

"She's in Wyoming. She's been in Wyoming for the last four years." As I explained what I learned and what I'd seen at her cabin, the family members had various reactions. Aster's was my favorite though because when she figured it out she started laughing. While my feelings for her had long since dissipated and I could see how perfect she was with Isaac, I still enjoyed her as a person. She always saw things differently.

"So tricky. And genius."

"We knew she was a genius," Owen adds, shaking his head. He looks amused as well but is holding it in like he holds everything in.

"If you know where she is, why did you leave?" Alina asks.

"Because you wanted me to find her, not kidnap her. She isn't ready."

"Ready to what?" Alina rolls her eyes. She's the one who hired me, the only living person who knows the darkest part of my background that qualified me to work for them, and I owe her so much. But sometimes she can be out of touch with emotions.

"It's complicated, Lina," I answer softly, thinking about everything Aspen said into the dark like she couldn't stop herself. Like she'd been waiting years to say some of those things and have someone hear them. "She's got a lot of baggage about all of you, and a lot she blames herself for. Aspen wants to be alone."

"Is she okay?" Anora asks, tears in her big eyes.

"Yeah, by most metrics. She's healthy, she has a house, a job, a dog named Troy. That's how I found her. Is she happy? I don't think so, but is she okay? Yeah." Giving them some of these details feels oddly disloyal, even though Aspen isn't the one I'm supposed to be loyal to.

Owen looks around the table. "Now what?"

"We convince her to come home," Aro says, but she's looking off into the middle distance, and Harp puts a hand on her thigh. Aro used to be so different, but after everything that happened she removed herself a little. While she was mad at me and blamed for a long time, I know that's done. We cleared the air and have a good relationship, but she's always frustrated with me because I never stopped blaming myself. Aro lives in the real middle of nowhere with Harp and Henry, and works as a part-time assassin. I never saw that coming.

"Let me," I offer. "I'm pretty sure she knows I found her and she hasn't gone running. The door is open. Give me a chance to convince her to come back."

"I'm pro-kidnapping," Alina responds with a shrug. "It's been four years. My patience is at zero."

"Your patience is always at zero," Aster drawls. "I'm team convince."

"Me too," Aro answers.

Anora stares at Owen, and they have a silent conversation across the table. "I'll give you a chance to convince her, but I expect her to come back with you one way or the other." Anora turns to me and her voice and face are hard, an expression rarely seen on her. "We have to finish this."

"I can do that." I could. I know that if I can't convince Aspen, I will get her in this house and I will make sure she has the opportunity to hash things out with her sisters. I will make sure that she has the chance to truly hear them that they don't blame her for anything.

I'll also help her get the hell out when it's done. There's nothing on earth that would convince me to tie her down or trap her anywhere after what she went through. Aspen deserves her freedom, even when I disagree with her reasons for thinking she needs it. Or for thinking that having her freedom means she can't have her family. Hopefully getting her back here helps her find the happy medium.

The group at the table breaks off to go find their respective children, and Owen gives me a nod telling me to go back to his office. I walk in that direction and hear him murmur something to his wife before following me.

"What didn't you say?" he asks as he closes the door behind us. The man's instincts are fucking gold. It's almost creepy.

"Someone else is looking for her. I had to pay the vet that found her $50k just to keep it between us. He gets the full payment, by the way." If I let him live. If he hasn't fucked this up.

"Consider it done." Owen pinches the bridge of his nose and takes a deep breath. "Are we going to have a problem, Gailen?"

"What kind of problem?"

"I know you've been chasing her for years. You probably know her better than any of us at this point. Is that going to be a problem?" Goddamn it. It's like he knew that my loyalty was shifting even before I did.

Yes. "No."

We stare each other down and I give him nothing.

"I'm protective of her," I finally admit. "I want her back here with you, but I also understand how much she's hurting and why she's afraid. I'll do what needs to be done."

Owen nods and sighs again, his perpetual state, and sits down at his desk. That's a good enough answer for now. I believe, even if it was against Anora's wishes, that Owen would let Aspen go if it was what she wanted and she wasn't in danger. He was trapped in his own kind of hell for a long time, and he needed to go be on his own before he could find his way home. He'll believe that Aspen deserves her space.

"Who's looking for her?"

"There's too many options. She's still hacking and working with her collective so they could've pissed someone off. Anyone on your end of things who knows about her? Leftovers from Elton?"

He shakes his head slowly. "Not that I know of, but we'll start watching. I'm sure Aster will be delighted when I ask her to drag up the Forresters again."

We both share a humorless laugh. Owen sobers and his eyes bore into mine.

"It's a job, Gailen, don't forget that."

No, Aspen is a person. Fuck, for the last four years chasing Aspen has been a way of life. A way for me to feel useful after recovering from my injuries. Chasing her gave me purpose. Maybe I am afraid of this ending because I have to figure out what to do with myself after that. I let her become an obsession because if she was only a job, it had an end date.

"I know."

He stares at me again. "Go get some rest, you look like shit."

I nod. "I'm heading back tomorrow." I would head back tonight if I thought I'd get enough sleep on the plane, but I need to be on my guard. I found Aspen, and it feels like I pulled a pin in a grenade and I'm waiting for the explosion. The itch in my gut to get back to her won't be settled easily. It's never been simple when it comes to Aspen and I doubt that's going to change.

8

Gailen

The second I get back into town, I go to Dr. Murray first to close the loop and pay the debt. I want to ensure his discretion.

Dr. Murray is at the front desk when I walk in and jumps a little when he sees me.

"Back again?" he forces a laugh. That motherfucker did something. I feel it in my bones.

"I wanted to complete our transaction."

"It was her? Who you were looking for?" His face pales underneath his beard like he wasn't expecting it to be true.

I don't like it, but I don't want to press him over nothing, not when I might need to break him later. Even though he offered medical services to people avoiding hospitals, that's different than potentially turning over a human being when they don't want to be found. I'm going to give him the benefit of the doubt that his fear is about that, rather than because he put his life at risk for twice the payout.

I don't answer him, and tap through the app on my phone that will transfer the remaining balance of the reward to his accounts.

"The money is yours. Forget you ever saw her."

He gulps. "You've got it."

I stare at him in warning for a long moment, until he nods again with more force. I have a feeling I'll be back. Without another word, I walk out the door and get in my current rental truck. The tires eat the pavement as I drive to Aspen's cabin.

It shouldn't feel like a huge relief when her Land Rover is still in the driveway. I hate feeling good about the fact that there's smoke coming from her chimney and it doesn't look like she's made any moves to run at all. I can't tell if I want the chase to continue, or if I'm that terrified of what I'll feel being in her presence. Aspen affects me.

It's useless to wish that she didn't, but I don't know if I'm prepared for it. It's been a long time since I felt anything but unrelenting determination. There wasn't room to feel other things while I was on the hunt, and that was the way I wanted it to be.

I park the truck and get out. Before I take more than a few steps, Aspen opens the front door and leans against the jamb with her arms crossed. Troy is a few steps behind her, dancing in excitement. Her face gives nothing away as she watches me approach. She's wearing a long-sleeved t-shirt and jean shorts that show off the golden tone of her skin. My eyes drop down and then back up her body before I can catch myself.

When my eyes meet Aspen's she's smirking, and not even remotely bothered by my perusal of her body. With slightly exaggerated motions, she cocks her head and lets her eyes drag along my form. I can feel myself getting hard under her gaze, and it only gets worse when I see her cheeks tint pink.

We affect *each other*.

That's even more dangerous.

Aspen takes a few steps back into the house and extends her arm. "Come on in, although I think you've been here before."

I don't rise to that. I'm not going to confirm that I was here, and that I remember every word she said in the dark. If I think about it too much, I'm going to start promising to keep her safe, and overwhelm her with the need to protect her. I'll tell her that I dream about her too, almost every night, and that saving her is the only thing keeping me going.

She's been an obsession for years, but everything about her was blurry. I was more obsessed with the concept than the actual person. Now that I'm starting to see the person, the obsession hasn't shifted at all. In person, she's even better.

The color of her skin. The tight, wiry muscles of her arms and legs. The way she only smiles with one side of her mouth and talks with a tone that's supposed to make you believe she's always bored. The shining darkness of her hair, and the unfathomable depth of her dark eyes. She might resemble her sisters in her facial features, but those eyes are pure Forrester. Elton had dark eyes too, but his were flat.

Aspen's dark eyes are infinite, full of so much that she's trying hard to hide. It's the only crack in her mask. She can't hide what her eyes are saying. Maybe I never felt like this because I never saw them clearly before. I couldn't see her soul in an image, but I can see it now. It's speaking to mine, even if I wish it wasn't.

I walk inside the house and look around like I've never seen it before. Aspen watches me and when she cackles with laughter I almost break and laugh too.

"Sit," she says as she waves toward the couch in front of the fireplace. "I've got pizza."

I watch her walk across the open room to the kitchen counter where a large pizza is cooling. All of her movements are precise but elegant, as if she's worked hard to have complete control over her body. Aspen gets out a pizza cutter and slices it into triangles. I prefer squares, but it doesn't seem relevant.

She carries the board with the cut pizza to the coffee table and sits down on the other end of the couch. We stare at each other.

Without breaking eye contact, she reaches over and grabs a slice, takes a bite, and then slowly chews it. It's another game. Who will look away first.

"Do you eat?" she asks after swallowing.

"I do, but I'm not sure what we're doing here."

"We're going to eat pizza, and talk about what happens next."

I nod and let her win by looking down to take a slice. We eat in silence, mostly staring at each other. It should be awkward or weird, but it's not. It's the first time we've ever been able to study one another in the flesh and we're both taking advantage of the moment. I can see her eyes picking up on details that wouldn't be in videos or photos, the same as I'm doing to her.

Aspen always wears her hair down, but when she tucks it behind her left ear I can see that she's got piercings going up the curve, at least 6. I wonder if the other ear is pierced too and have to quench my desire to reach out and tuck the hair on the right. It would be dangerous if I touched her.

There are scars on her that I can see now: on the right side of her jaw - a little curve that's a slightly lighter color than the skin around it, another going into her hairline almost dead center of her forehead, and a last one just below her left eye. It looks like a puncture. I don't know what her brother did to her, but I suddenly wish I could hear him burning alive again. I wish I could play his screams for her so she would know he died in agony and was punished for what he'd done.

Aspen's eyes are hungry as she looks at me. I want to crawl inside her mind and know what she's thinking and why. For the first time in my life, I actually care what someone thinks of me. I want to know how she sees me, and how she feels about the pull that keeps building between us. Does she want it, or does she want to fight it like I do?

She burrows down further into the couch and pats the space between us. Troy jumps up and snuggles against her body. He looks at me like

I'm a friend but the arrangement of his body makes it clear he's there to take care of her. I like that she had a friend, for however long she's had him. It was concerning to think of her alone for so long at such a young age.

"I don't want to go to them."

"I know."

She frowns at my response. "But I'm done running. I'm tired." I can hear it in her voice and my chest throbs in response. My arms almost lift to reach for her.

"They aren't trying to trap you," I tell her honestly. "I know that's what you've known, but give them a chance."

"I don't deserve a chance." Her voice is so fucking small it hurts.

"You do. You deserve to move on and be a part of a family that wants you."

She shakes her head and buries her hand in Troy's fur for comfort.

"They've moved on with their lives. They need to move on from what happened, and me being there will bring all of it up again. I will be a constant reminder of their pain."

"And of your own."

Aspen glares at me for calling her out. "We all deserve to move on."

I meet her eyes, challenging that statement, and she breaks away from me to stare at the fire.

"Have you moved on, Aspen?" She twitches, then meets my gaze again.

"Have you, Gailen?" I twitch too, and I realize it's because she said my name. I've never heard her say it before, and my dick really likes it. I want to hear her say it in every possible tone and inflection, even angry, but especially with pleasure.

"No," I answer honestly. "I need closure, and I can only get it from you."

"About what?" She frowns. I shrug in response because we're

37

not there yet. We might never be there. Silence falls again, but it's contemplative rather than tense. It's hard to believe how relaxed I feel in this moment, sitting quietly with Aspen, listening to the dog huff and the fire crack. Like I've finally found peace.

I wonder if it's because I found her, or because it's just her.

"Convince me," she says softly.

I turn to look at her, and tilt my head in question.

"Stay and convince me that they have room for me. That me seeing them and building a relationship with them is the healthy thing for any of us."

I nod immediately. "I can do that."

One side of Aspen's mouth kicks up in a smile. "Okay then."

9

Aspen

To make some space between us, I get the pizza leftovers from the coffee table and waste time in the kitchen. Gailen hasn't taken his eyes off me, as if watching me is fascinating. I'm his favorite show, apparently. Then again, given the way we've done nothing but watch each other for years it shouldn't be surprising.

I didn't expect to feel like this and I don't know what to do about it.

When I was younger and less self-aware, because I'm almost too self-aware now, in that hospital in New York, I absolutely had a crush on Gailen. He was the big, strong man that carried me through literal fire. Who got hurt to save me. Not to mention, he's pretty as fuck. Even with the too long hair and the scruff he needs to shave, Gailen is nice to look at.

His lips are a little too big for his face, thick, soft, and pink, while the rest of him is all hard lines and angles, a jaw sharp enough to cut, a nose that's a straight aristocratic slope, and honey brown eyes that see too damn much. Being in proximity to his body is hazardous to my own. I react to him in ways I wasn't expecting. Like when I could feel him close to me the other night without seeing him.

That shouldn't be real. But I know that he could move silently around this house and I would know where he was in proximity to me. Like I'm a compass and he's true north. Whichever way he turns, my arrow follows.

I can't imagine that he feels the same way.

I'm not a kid, I've never been a kid, and I've shown Gailen and the Sorrelles repeatedly that I'm smart and can take care of myself.

But.

I'm still 9 years younger than him.

I might as well be ancient with all I've been through and survived, but some people won't see it as a matter of our minds and maturity.

If I made a move on him, would he reciprocate? I haven't had sex in almost 2 years and being so close to him is making me ache in parts I'm very good at ignoring. My palms itch with the desire to touch his skin.

I didn't think he'd agree to my demand to stay here. I've always kind of assumed he had some sort of life to get back to, but maybe not. I'm used to not being worth anyone's time and effort, so I requested something I thought he would reject.

Gailen acts as if he has the patience to sit here and convince me when it's a lost cause. There's nothing I can think of that he could say that would make me believe going to the Sorrelles was the right thing to do, let alone something they truly wanted. I know they're good people and they feel obligated to take care of me. They aren't.

I'm fine on my own. Gailen can help me figure out how to make them understand that. They are not obligated to me, and they are not letting anyone down by leaving me to my own devices. It's an act of love for me to let them go.

Honestly, I was hoping my demand that he stay would force some kind of confrontation so I could ask him to leave. Delay the only two possible outcomes: he kidnaps me, or he leaves. The only way I'm going to Chicago is by force. I'm smart enough to know that my estranged family can be ruthless when they want to be. They didn't spend all that money to chase me to let me get away.

"Listen, this is pointless." Time for another tactic. "I'm not going to get pulled into the fantasy of these little do-gooders that I'm their long lost sister. This is all fake so they can feel better about themselves and never have to reveal to their children they let their bastard sibling run off. The point has been made, they can say that I rejected them, and move on." My limbs were getting tight and stiff with each word I spoke; I didn't believe most of it and even voicing it made me feel kind of sick.

"I'm a grumpy jerk who likes to live alone, does highly illegal things on the internet, and prefers her dog for company. There will be no hugs, no teary reunion, no gratitude on my part. Tell them to let me go."

Rant complete, I look up at Gailen to find him smiling at me. It's disarming, and I freeze.

"Please, tell me more." His voice is sarcastic, but also amused.

"They're all married with kids and lives. I'm a bump in the road."

"Don't you want to know where you come from?" His face falls a little.

"I know. I know who they are, I know who he was." We both know the "he" I'm referring to is Don Sorrelle. "I know that it will never outweigh what I grew up with. I'm not good. I'll never be good."

He snorts. "Now you sound like Aster."

I flinch at that.

"Did you really walk away from them, Aspen? You ran, never looked back, never wondered, built your life, never spared your family a thought, huh?"

"Of course." Liar.

"Liar." He stands up and walks over to me, leaning on his hands on the other side of the counter. "If that was true, you wouldn't have sent me on a wild goose chase for the last four years. If you didn't care, your conscience wouldn't have kept prodding you to send up a signal and let them know you're alive. I wouldn't be here right now."

We stare at each other and I know he won't back down.

"All I've ever done is hurt them."

His face falls in sympathy. "That's not how they see it."

"They should. Everything that happened to them back then was possible because of me."

"You didn't have a choice."

"There's always a choice," I snap back.

"When you're an adult, yes. But for you? It was compliance or death, Aspen. They would rather you be alive." We stare at each other again and I don't know if I agree with his statement. For a few years there it was pretty dodgy about whether or not I wanted to be alive. I had to really work to believe that surviving was the better option. Sometimes I think I live just to spite my dead asshole brother.

"They're more forgiving than you can imagine." Gailen swallows heavily. "I'm the reason Don is dead, and they've all forgiven me."

I stare at him for a moment and wonder if he's serious. If he really takes the blame for that day on himself. The long lines of his face and the apology in his eyes confirm that he really thinks its his fault.

No matter how I try, I can't stop myself from bursting out laughing.

10

Gailen

Well, that wasn't the reaction I was expecting.

Aspen is laughing so hard she has to put her head down on her arms on the counter. When she looks up again, there are tears streaming down her face. I go to move around the counter but she holds out a hand to stop me, and waves me away.

"Gailen." She takes a deep breath and wipes her face. "Nothing you could have done that day would've stopped what happened. The only difference is that you'd be dead."

Offense punches me in the gut. "I would have protected Don."

"I believe that you would have tried, but I picked Shadow for a reason."

I still. "What?"

"Elton made me choose. I did the research. I made the call. Someone quick and absolutely deadly." She shivers and I want to move to her and move past her resistance, take her in my arms and make her feel safe. "I wanted it to be fast. So I picked Shadow."

"Aspen," I try but I don't know what else to say.

"That's why I can't go back. It's not just the trouble I caused for Designation, or helping him hide us and the money, it's that I was an active part of the choices that led to their father's death, and harmed their well-being."

"He was your father too."

She shakes her head sharply, rejecting that.

"Do you think they don't know? Do you really believe with all that you know about them, they don't know all of this already? They know it all and they want you anyway."

Aspen ignores my question. "I killed their father. Shadow would've killed you, and then Shadow got obsessed with Aro. That's all my fault."

"I'm still here, but I should have been there. It was my job."

She stares at me for a long time. "You would've died. Then who would've saved me?"

I snort. "Anora, without question. Owen was holding her back when I walked out with you."

Aspen reacts to that, stepping back as if I've pushed her. She really doesn't understand the depth and dedication of her sisters when it comes to her.

"I'm glad you're not dead." Her voice is quiet and sad.

I shake my head at her, because sometimes I think it would be better to feel nothing than to feel all this guilt that eats me alive. If I'd died saving her, I wouldn't be here, feeling like a debt was still owed, like my life wasn't my own.

Except the more I'm with Aspen, the more those feelings are morphing inside me into something else.

"Is that why you're staying away? Because you think if they know the truth they'll hate you?" I ask her, trying to be blunt and get to the heart of it.

"They will."

"No," I shake my head sharply. "They will never give up on you."

A tear falls down Aspen's cheek. "*You* never gave up on me. It's not the same."

11

Aspen

I've always asked myself why he won't give up. Why they never gave up.

There is nothing about me to save. There is nothing to be redeemed. I was raised by a monster and a woman too afraid to do anything about it. I couldn't save her, and I couldn't save myself. Elton raised me to be his twisted, obedient minion and that's exactly what I was until Anora.

Anora didn't save me, she freed me, but it changed nothing about the fundamental reality of who I was shaped to be. I hurt people to stop myself from getting hurt.

I'm still a little gremlin, curled up in the dark, waiting for an opportunity to wreak havoc even if that's not my intention. It's what I was made for. Even though my collective online mostly does things that we think are morally right, I genuinely believe I'm not capable of doing true good. The darkness inside me will always win. I'll always take it too far.

The only good thing I ever did was helping the Sorrelles rescue Anora.

But even then, when we knew they were coming, I ran with Elton.

I ran with him because that's what I knew. It was familiar to serve my brother, even when he hurt me, even when he starved me. The unknown was more frightening than the monster. I knew what Elton's punishments would be and that I could survive them.

It took me a long time to recognize how deep his abuse went. The fact that basic hygiene was a reward for good behavior, that I had to thank him for every scrap of food and if I didn't express enough gratitude he would take it away. The beatings, the abuse, the threats if I didn't do exactly what he wanted, or if I voiced an opinion. There was always a reason for him to abuse me.

Yet, I stayed. I ran with him. He said jump and I did it without needing to ask how high.

I tried to stay inside that burning house to die with him because I was afraid of what the world would do to me without him. He had so thoroughly terrified me of all the things I didn't know that I would rather have died than learn about it. I believed that I was only fit to die.

Now, I hate that I ever felt that way. The world was so much easier than I expected it to be. I had two things that made it easy to maneuver: a lot of money, and an appearance of innocence. People wanted to help me, and I let them. I was canny enough to know the ones that wanted to take advantage of me and avoid them. It was like a scent that only they had, and I'd grown up knowing what it was.

Corruption smelled like sweet rot. Too much, and too strong.

It's probably a scent that clings to me, too. Corrupted, rotting, ruining.

"I can't let what I am touch them," I admit softly. It's easy to be open with Gailen. It feels like we're continuing a conversation.

"What are you?"

"Infectious." I bite my lip but continue. "I'll ruin them."

"They've been ruined before, and they came back stronger than ever. You met them, but you don't know them."

"I don't deserve to know them." That's the truth. I don't deserve their forgiveness, their openness, their care, or their understanding. I don't deserve to stand in the house their father built, the house he died in, and feel even a teaspoon of love from them.

They will tell me that he would've loved me. They'll tell me that I can still have the life I would have if he'd known about me, but that isn't true. There's no going back, and there's no fixing me. I can't move forward on their terms, and they would overrule me. They would pull me in with their determination and goodness and I think it would kill me a little bit every day.

They'd try to give me back an innocence that I never had a chance to possess. For them it would be an act of love because they can't see the monster beneath my skin.

I'd be put into a box that I don't want to fit.

The broken one, the one that needs to be healed, the one that needs to change. I hate how I got here, but I don't want to change who I am now. The world is a weird, chaotic place and I figured out who I am inside of it without anyone beside me. Without anyone's perspectives pressuring me.

It was me who decided where I lived, what I do, what I believe. It was me who decided when I was ready for therapy. That decided there was nothing wrong with taking a shower every day, sometimes more than once a day, that overcame my food insecurities, that goes into the city once a month to get waxed because I'm disgusted by my own body hair. It was me that decided that was a trauma response I could live with. I was the one that decided I didn't care about being a criminal, and that I believed in chaotic good.

I don't care how I do it as long as I'm doing it for the right reasons.

I can't be a Sorrelle. I can't be someone that people watch, pay attention to, have an opinion about. I like my anonymity and I want to keep it. I wasn't raised to be seen. I was raised to crawl in the small spaces behind the world.

Hiding keeps me sane, and I want to keep doing it.

"The only reason I'm entertaining this conversation is because I owe you my life." I meet Gailen's golden gaze, and feel my body melt. I hate that I react to him so strongly but even with only this short time in each other's proximity, he's in my veins. The hum of his presence is moving beneath my skin.

"You owe me nothing." He sounds sincere.

I shake my head. "I would have let myself die without you. I was ready to do that."

"I know."

"Did you ever tell them?"

He shakes his head. "I heard you. In the hospital."

My entire body goes cold. The night I ran away, I asked Anora and Owen if I could see Gailen. We were supposed to be leaving for Chicago the next day, and even though I knew that I was going to run and the plan was already in place, I needed to see him. The man who had saved me when I thought I didn't want to be saved. The man I was sure would believe he'd made a mistake when he woke up and found that I'd run anyway.

I remember clearly leaning over his injured, unconscious form and whispering in his ear.

I am so sorry. You didn't have to do this. Please don't tell them.

Then I'd kissed his cheek, giving in to something I didn't understand. I never thought I'd see him again.

"It was between you and me. It still is. It always will be." Gailen's hand lifts like he's going to touch me, and then it drops. It fists at his side, knuckles white. He's trying so hard to control himself.

There I go, turning into a puddle again, because that does something to me. The idea that there are already intimate secrets between us is heady. My clit throbs and my nipples tighten. My body wants to press against his body, show him physically how much everything he says affects me, but my brain is screaming at me not to be an idiot.

"Let me go. Go back to your life." I only half mean it.

"What life?" Gailen pushes away from the counter and turns his back to me, looking out the large front windows of the house. His body is tense, and I feel like he's mentally talking himself out of whatever he wants to say.

I stare at his back and wonder about his scars. I wonder if he'll want to see mine.

"I can't let you go, Aspen Sorrelle. I can't." Gailen's voice is quiet and distraught, and I'm glad I can't see his face. I don't think I could handle the expression.

"It's Forrester."

He turns around then, derision on his face. "No, it isn't. You deserve your father's name because despite your denials, I see all of them in you. I see him in you."

I have nothing to say to that. Part of me wants him to say more about that, but I also know how much it would hurt. Don is the blind spot of my information. I couldn't bring myself to learn much about him.

"I'm going to stay, and I'm going to convince you that you can be as isolated as you want but you don't have to be alone." Gailen steps close again and catches my jaw, running his thumb over my cheek.

I want to climb him like a tree. I can't recall the last time I was touched by another person. My mouth gapes slightly at the feeling, and I just know that I'm looking at him with stars in my eyes. He's perfect. Visually, personally, he is everything that makes my mind and body go haywire. Parts of me I didn't even know existed are awake and aware.

"Fine."

12

Gailen

Touching her was a mistake. That one brush of my thumb and feeling the solid warmth of her radiated through my entire body. It was like that was the confirmation I needed that she was real, and that all of this wasn't a very convincing figment of my imagination.

Broken, beautiful, impressive Aspen Sorrelle is the greatest danger I've ever faced. Aspen feels inevitable.

I want to take on all her pain, her regrets, all of the destructive thoughts that she has. They can live inside me and kill me if it means they are no longer holding her down. Honestly, if it takes the rest of my life to convince her to open the door to her family, that's fine with me. I don't want to leave her side.

This is where it was always leading me.

I don't want it, but I can't deny it.

The search for Aspen was about more than redemption, it was about finding my home. Hours in her presence and I feel more at ease in my body than I have, maybe, ever. Even before the fire, I never felt comfortable in my skin, and the scar only made it worse. Now that all feels irrelevant.

I see the way she looks at me.

Aspen walks around me and Troy trots after her toward the front door.

"We're going for a walk."

I shrug and follow them. Aspen won't be able to avoid the conversation forever, but I'll take it at her pace.

We wander through the field behind her house, and Aspen throws a toy for Troy to fetch. I love watching her body move and her obvious strength. She can hold her own.

I want to get my hands on her and feel it for myself.

"So, tell me about these illegal internet things."

Aspen laughs, and it's a surprisingly free sound if a little bit rusty. Like it doesn't happen often.

"I work with a collective. We generally get paid to help bad people take down other bad people, but it always circles back around. Our only loyalty is to each other."

"Have you ever met them?"

"Yes," Aspen answers but she's blushing. I don't want to know, even as jealousy punches me in the gut. "They helped me when I was running."

"That explains a lot."

Troy brings the toy back but comes to me instead of Aspen. I squat down and pet him, praising him for being a good boy, and he drops the toy between us as his tongue lolls out. I dig my hands into the fluffy scruff around his neck and scratch him.

"Where'd you get him?" I ask her.

"There's a farmers market in town sometimes and someone was giving away puppies. We met eyes and I knew he was mine."

"Why Troy?"

Aspen blushes again and doesn't answer me. I give her time, and stand up with Troy's toy. I tease him with it, and then send it flying across the field. Troy goes bounding through the grass after it. When I look at Aspen out of the corner of my eye, she's smiling as she watches him run. He gets distracted from the toy by some birds, and goes running off in another direction.

"One of the collective is a Disney adult. I had a lot to catch up on, and when I stayed with her we watched basically non-stop Disney. I liked High School Musical." The embarrassment in her voice is obvious, and the blush on her cheeks deepens.

"You named your dog after Zac Efron?"

She shrugs, and kneels down as Troy finally comes running back to us.

"What else did you catch up on?"

"A lot of television, a few movies. The collective has a list and I make my way through it. I don't like reading as much, I'm too slow, but I can watch anything." She throws the toy and starts walking, as if staying still is adding to her discomfort. "Right now I'm watching Avatar."

"The blue people or the Last Airbender?"

Aspen scoffs. "The Last Airbender."

"If I ever had a pet, I'd name it Appa. It doesn't get cooler than a flying sky bison."

"True." Aspen turns and starts walking in another direction, and I follow. That's our entire relationship so far; she goes, I follow, and hopefully I catch up.

"Can I watch it with you tonight?"

"Just don't spoil anything."

I make a motion on my chest to cross my heart, and she looks confused.

"Crossing my heart. It's making a promise."

"Oh. I'll have to Google that. I didn't know that was a thing."

Even though she's been out in the world for years, there's so much about growing up and being exposed to other people that she never got to experience. Little things that everyone knows that she doesn't. It's more than movies, shows, and books. It's anachronisms and language, small motions that communicate something to most people that mean nothing to her. I want to know what else she doesn't know, and I want to teach her.

"Are you happy?" That was Anora's question, and even though I knew the answer, I wanted to hear it from Aspen.

"What's happy? What does happy feel like?" She throws up her arms. "Am I happier than I was growing up, absolutely. Am I content with my life, do I feel fulfilled? Most of the time, yeah. What does happy matter, then? I'm alive, I'm free. That's enough."

If she believed that, I was going to be glad to prove her wrong.

I wanted her happy. I wanted that laugh to be familiar and common. That smile to be on her face because she looked at her life and liked what she saw because of what was in it, not because of what wasn't.

Aspen was still living under the shadow of her brother's sins.

"Let me take you to dinner. Drive you into town, eat food we didn't cook, and then we can get a pie and watch Avatar. Deal?"

"Are you asking me on a date, Gailen Burke?"

For some reason it surprises me that she knows my last name, and makes me wonder what else she knows about me. That's a conversation we'll have because seeing it on paper isn't the same as hearing it from me. Aspen has earned my past. I put my hands in my pockets and glance over at her.

"Do you want it to be?"

Aspen doesn't answer. She whistles for Troy and walks back toward the house. I follow, and watch her put the dog in his crate.

"Let's go."

Aspen sets the security system and locks the door of the cabin. She pulls something up on her phone and I see camera feeds. It doesn't surprise me that she has a very thorough, nearly invasive, system set up where she lives but a lot of it is focused inside rather than out. I'd gotten around the cameras and the system when I came here the first time, but I wonder if she'd been able to confirm it was me through some measure that I missed. I'll ask her about it later.

I open the door of my truck for her and try not to linger on her legs as she climbs in.

"How mad were you when you realized I was never on the run?" She asks after 10 minutes of silence. I look over at her but she's staring out the window, a hint of a blush on her cheeks. In all my chasing, I never imagined she'd have such a lack of a poker face. Everything she's feeling shows, especially because she blushes so easily.

"Honestly? I was kind of impressed. More amused than angry, even. Owen said you're a genius and you proved him right."

"Really? You don't...resent me?"

That makes me think for a moment. I don't resent Aspen. Hunting her had given me a purpose for the last 4 years and helped my recovery in both mental and physical ways. Knowing that she was doing it to make sure we knew she was alive, even if it was all a game, isn't something that makes me angry. It makes me feel relieved.

"No. It helped me. It forced you to keep contact with us in one way or another. I don't resent how you chose to deal or keep yourself safe."

"I don't understand," she says softly. We drop into silence again for the rest of the drive, and when I park in a spot outside the local diner neither of us makes a move to leave the truck.

I take a deep breath. "I understand what it's like to want two opposing things at the same time. You wanted to run and hide, but you also didn't want to burn the bridge. I could never be angry with you for trying to take care of yourself in a way that made sense to you."

She turns to look at me and assess if I'm being honest with her. After a penetrating look she huffs and rolls her eyes. I laugh and she does too as we get out of the truck.

The diner is seat yourself, so we take a booth in the back corner and start looking through the menu. As she reads, I look around the semi-full restaurant. There's a table of three men in the back, and one of them keeps glancing over at us. They don't have the same vibe as the people I assume are locals. They're in nicer clothing, and it's in better shape. Most of the local people are blue collar, or ranchers and farmers, and their clothes reflect it.

These guys are too clean.

I don't like it, but they make no move to come near us. I'll have to keep watching to see if it's a problem, or just my instincts and desire to protect Aspen going into overdrive.

"What are you having? Burger?"

"I don't eat meat."

"Then what was the sausage on the pizza today?"

She smirks at me. "Well-seasoned tofu."

I blink a few times in surprise. "I had no idea. When did you decide that?"

"Well, I had very little idea how to cook, and it felt wrong to put more pain into the world when I've already been part of so much. Vegetarianism felt right to me."

That's oddly sweet. "Do you mind if I eat meat?"

"Nope. To each their own." Before she could say more, the waitress stops by our table. Aspen's orders a breakfast spread of eggs and pancakes, and I get a cheeseburger with waffle fries. I love diner food and I have no doubt this will hit the spot.

We keep talking about other choices she made for herself as she explored her freedom. The clothes she wanted to wear, her hair, even the colors of the throw pillows and the bedding in her room.

"People take choices for granted. We make a million little ones every day and some that are probably so insignificant to a normal person are huge to me. The first time I bought grape jelly for my toast, I cried." She laughs and shakes her head. The desire to touch and reassure her makes my hands shake.

We eat as we talk, and I wonder if she realizes how lonely she's been. I barely say a word as Aspen jumps from subject to subject, motor-mouthing like she's going to run out of time, or I'm going to cut her off. I would never.

I order us a strawberry rhubarb pie to go, and the server also gives us a tub of their homemade whipped cream.

By the time we're done, the men I was worried about have left the diner, and I saw them get in an SUV and drive away. Still, I watch for them on the drive back and keep a vigilant watch for anyone following us. Aspen drifts off to sleep mid-word talking about the first time she voted last year.

I am afraid that I'm already half in love with this wild, determined woman. I never thought I'd have feelings like that again, let alone for another Sorrelle, and definitely not for Aspen. I didn't think I saw her as more than a job, not until I was in her presence. It's like everything I thought I knew shifted, and I'm adjusting to this new reality where all I want is what will make Aspen happy.

Dangerous fucking territory. Owen is going to kick my ass.

13

Aspen

If this is a date, there's never been a better one. Not only did Gailen listen to me like I had something worth saying, when we got back to my cabin we sat on the couch and ate the pie straight out of the pan with two forks. We watched Avatar and laughed and argued, and it felt like it was how we spent every night. It felt like he'd always been with me.

I lean back on my big fat couch and hold my overly full stomach. Gailen pauses the show when my blinks get too long.

"I think we need to call it."

"Okay. Are you alright crashing on the couch? It's long enough and I've got plenty of blankets." I don't think either of us are in a place for what I really want, which is to ask him to come bed with me. Not to do anything more than sleep, but there's an intimacy line we'd be crossing. Plus, it would hurt like hell if he rejected me even if he thought he was doing it for my own good.

"The couch is fine." He moves toward his bag by the door, and I leave him to it as I go upstairs and grab a sheet, a pillow, and a thick down comforter. It gets cold out here in the winters and after too many years of freezing my ass off, I love to have so many layers I melt. It'll be warm enough for a summer evening.

Gailen is still in the bathroom when I go downstairs, so I make up the couch for him. I face his head away from the front door because it seems like the kind of thing he'd think about. I'd give him access to the cameras if he asked.

I hear the door open and turn around just as I get the blanket settled. He's wearing fitted gray sweatpants and a black t-shirt. It shows off his fit body and the tattoos on his arms. His feet are bare and I find them oddly sexy. The veins are obvious along the top of his foot and it feels almost like seeing him naked. Gailen is a soldier. He's always dressed, always ready, and now he's dressed down in front of me.

He tucks a toiletry bag into his pack and steps closer to me.

I awkwardly indicate the sofa. "There's a plug on the floor under the table if you need to charge your phone."

"Thanks. Would you give me access to the cameras?"

I bite my lips to hide my smile, and hold my hand out for his phone. It takes me a moment to download my app to his phone and put in login information. I don't tell him that he's got his own username and password. He has since I setup the system. I couldn't explain why except that it felt like someday this moment would come.

When he takes the phone back, he flips through the cameras and his eyebrows raise.

"That was more than I thought there was."

I grin. "Good."

I take a step to move around him and our bodies brush. Tension ricochets through me and I stop, looking up at his face. Gailen's eyes are tracing over me as if he's trying to memorize me. As if he thinks I'm going to go away. I'm caught now. I won't run again.

"See you in the morning," I say softly, squeezing my thighs together. I've had fun with my body with others, but I've never wanted anyone the way that I want him. My body sways as if trying to get closer, and

Gailen leans in return.

"Sweet dreams, Aspen." His mouth is close enough to mine that I can feel his breath. After a tense moment he steps to the side, breaking us apart. I let out a harsh breath and keep walking until I'm up the stairs and into the loft that serves as my bedroom. Troy follows behind me and gets comfortable on the bed.

There's no door, just a long hallway and walls, but I think I could be quiet enough that he wouldn't hear me if I needed to get off. It seems unlikely that I'll be able to sleep with this much tension and arousal coursing through my body.

My imagination plays out how the rest of our moment could've gone. I imagine Gailen crashing his lips to mine, grabbing my body with his big, strong hands, hard enough to leave marks. Reminders that he touched me. When I think about touching him over his sweatpants, I slide my hand inside my shorts and touch myself. I'm already soaked, my clit sensitive and ready, but I can't picture his dick. I get too caught up trying to think about it, and I lose the momentum building toward an orgasm.

I sigh and take my hand out of my shorts.

My brain will get too focused on the details because the real thing is so close by. He's right there. I could yell and we'd be able to carry on a conversation from our respective beds.

I breathe sharply as my heart starts racing. So much of my life was wasted and taken away from me that I've tried to live it with some verve. I rarely deny myself anything because the things I want are often small to most people. Gailen is the biggest, craziest thing I've ever wanted, and I don't think I should hold back.

It takes me another few minutes to convince myself, but I crawl out of bed and walk down the hall toward the landing.

And nearly bump into Gailen.

He's dressed and wearing his pack. My heart starts racing for totally different reasons.

Gailen holds a finger to his lips, and then asks very quietly, "You got a go bag?"

I don't roll my eyes like I want to, I just nod and turn away from him. It's easy to shift into defensive mode and I change clothes quickly. I pack the few things in my go-bag that are always with me, and I hook Troy by the collar.

A siren blips twice in the house, and Gailen comes into my bedroom. I'd really been wishing for that to happen under different circumstances.

He's already got the cameras up on his phone.

"There's a staircase out that door," I point. "Secondary egress."

Gailen's cheek lifts slightly. He pulls a gun from a holster on his back.

"Hold Troy. Follow me."

I hook my fingers through Troy's collar. He's been trained for this. Troy sticks close to me and we quietly slip down the stairs and hide in the shadows of the side of the house.

Gailen and I watch the front cameras as a team of men appear within range of its view.

"You trust me?" he asks softly.

"Yes." He might be the only person in the world that I do, and I have no idea why.

14

Gailen

I grab Aspen's hand in mine and start moving around the house as we watch the men move to the front door on the camera. They're sloppy and definitely underestimating Aspen; there's a chance they have no idea who I am. If it was me, and my former team, I'd be having them fan out around the house to watch all possible means to exit.

These guys are planning on busting in the front door and thinking they'll catch us unaware. Whoever sent them can't hire or train quality mercs for shit.

"Do you have your keys?"

Aspen shakes her head. "There's a spare key in the Land Rover, and there are other supplies in the back. I'm always ready to run."

Despite what we're facing, I smile and shake my head at her. She's perfect.

"When they go inside, we run. You drive, you know the area better. Head toward a city."

Aspen squeezes my hand in confirmation as we move to the corner of the house. The men are talking to each other and then take up a formation. I watch as they kick in the door and set off the alarm, probably hoping to cause panic and bad decision making. We're steps ahead of them already.

When all three of them step inside the cabin, I tug her with me and we run for the Land Rover. Aspen opens the driver's side door and Troy hops in and immediately goes to the backseat. We climb inside and put our bags in the back, then silently close the doors of the car. She had the inside lights turned off, and her level of preparation for something like this concerns me.

It's one thing to have a go bag and a plan to run, but this is beyond thorough.

Does she know who sent these guys? Does Aspen have some idea who's after her?

We watch, and when the men step deeper into the house, I nod at her to go.

Aspen starts the car and whips it around, pressing hard on the gas and sending the gravel of her driveway flying. There's a shout behind us but we're already halfway down the drive.

It's telling that they don't fire at us, which makes me believe they want Aspen alive. That's both a good and bad thing. Good because it means they'll be careful with force, but bad because it means they want something from her. I don't ever want my girl captured and forced to do anything ever again.

My heart is racing and I watch behind us and wait for the team to regroup. It doesn't take long before headlights appear in the distance.

"Turn off the headlights. Make a random turn. We'll figure out where we are when we lose them."

Aspen does what I say and turns onto a random farm road that disappears into a copse of trees. The headlights following us get closer and I watch as they drive past the road entirely.

"Where should we go?"

I shake my head at her because I need to process things for a moment. It's almost midnight but I know what I need to do. I make a call.

The phone rings twice before Aster answers.

"What?" I can tell by her tone that she wasn't sleeping, so she's regular grumpy instead of being woken up grumpy.

"Someone is after Aspen. 3 guys busted into her place. We got away, but someone else is looking for her."

"I'll start searching. Where are you going?"

"Don't know yet."

There's silence on the other end of the phone and I can almost hear her rolling her eyes.

"You know what you should do."

"Absolutely not!" Aspen blurts out. "I'm not dragging them into this."

"I'll let you know what I find. Keep us in the loop." Aster ends the call before I can say anything else, and without responding to Aspen's resistance.

"Let's head East," I finally decide and pull up a random city about two hours from here on my phone GPS.

"Can you drive?" Aspen's voice is timid and I'm worried, but we have to get somewhere safe before I can do much about that.

As we get out and move around the front of the car, Aspen crashes into me instead of going around me. Her arms wrap around my waist and before I know it, I'm hugging her back. She has her face buried in my chest and I can feel how fast and unsteady she's breathing.

The adrenaline crash is hitting her, and now she's getting upset. We left behind her home, and even though on one level she was ready to leave it in a moment, it's not the same as it actually happening.

Time passes as her breathing slows and some of the tension drops out of her body. She lets me go, and I hesitate to drop my arms but I follow her lead. We get in the car, back in moving forward mode. I start the route and we drive in silence. It's not tense, it's sad more than anything, but I have no doubt that when Aspen needs to talk, she'll talk to me.

15

Aspen

When my heart stops racing, my body starts shaking. When the shaking fades away, I'm left with an exhaustion I haven't experienced in a long time. The kind of thing that makes you feel like you'll never be rested again. Everything I've built is gone.

I remote wiped my computers while we were waiting for the men to go inside the house. They'll find nothing worthwhile. Nothing to them, but everything to me. The things that I used to mark my time and progress since I've been on my own.

Even though I know that I shouldn't, I pull up my cameras. I'm watching three men destroy my home without a second thought.

They shred my pillows and furniture, and knock my shelves over as they look for hiding spots they won't find. I can't look away when they knock a glass ornament off the shelf and it shatters. The first present I ever got from anyone that Si bought me on one of their trips to Disney.

Gailen can see what I'm doing but he doesn't stop me either. Maybe he's like me and he has to see the horror for himself before his brain can truly process it. We don't turn away. We watch until it's done and let it burn through us.

When I try to grab onto logic, I didn't lose anything I can't replace. I have the important things, I have Troy, I'm alive, and everything I had on my computers is backed up many times over. There are no items from my family or heirlooms, just the tokens that have value to me.

I lost the first things I got for myself.

I'm watching men who don't even know me, who have been paid to hunt me, destroy the dream I built for myself. It's a harsh lesson after so many years of feeling safe enough that I was actually never safe at all. It was a reminder I needed. Safety is an illusion.

I trust Gailen to keep me alive, but no one can truly keep me safe.

"You have to stop," he says softly. "I'm sorry."

"How...how did this happen?" It's been a long, long time since I cried because I'm scared, but if this situation might be worth the tears. The lump in my throat and the burning in my eyes are unfamiliar and uncomfortable.

"The vet called me. He mentioned someone else was looking, and I'm guessing he didn't keep your whereabouts to himself. I'll deal with him later."

"It's not worth it. People are selfish and choose to be oblivious. Don't punish him for human nature."

"Your cynicism is noted, but that's not why. Someone is only as good as their word, and his isn't worth anything. If I don't show the consequences for betraying us, others will."

I shake my head. This world that I was born into is a weird place; the rich and the criminals, the ones who have to worry about their reputation as much as their actions. Threats are everywhere to them, and minimizing the size of those threats is what they care about. It's frustrating but understandable.

My brain wants to cut ties and walk away, leave people behind and to their own devices, but Gailen sees it differently. Fine.

"I'm not going to Chicago." I know that might seem like the best next step, but I can't afford to be thrown off right now by the emotional turmoil of being with the Sorrelles.

"I know. Until we know what's going on, I think staying on the move is our best option. But, we should kind of circle the area. We have resources there."

"*You* have resources there."

"*We*. We'll keep going East."

"I'm not putting them in danger."

"What if the danger is because of them, not because of you?"

I frown at him. "Who even knows I exist?"

He nods, biting his bottom lip as he thinks. It's a weird time to find that sexy.

"Not many people. Still, I'm not ruling out going to your sisters if that's the best tactical decision. I promise you, if I think we can keep you and them safer by keeping you apart, that's what we'll do. Do you believe me?"

I stare out into the dark and consider his words. I do trust Gailen, and I know he's trying to be gentle about my relationship with the Sorrelles. I want to believe that he wouldn't force me into being around them unless it was the best decision. That he wouldn't use this as an excuse to get me where they want me.

For a second, it occurs to me that this could be a setup. That Gailen hired these men to attack us so we're forced to go on the run and forced to rely on the Sorrelles for protection. My stomach pits and I feel sick, a cold sweat breaking out all over my body.

Troy whimpers from the backseat, reacting to the quick and violent change of my mood and body chemistry. He pushes his face between us and rests his chin on my shoulder. I lean into his warm fur and dirty doggy smell, reassuring myself with something familiar.

"What's the matter?"

"If I asked you to separate right now, would you let me?"

The car jerks as Gailen flinches on the wheel. "Why would we do that?"

"Just…if I said I wanted to go on my own, would you let me?"

I'm surprised when Gailen pulls the car over. We're in the middle of nowhere and the only light is from the dashboard of the car. He looks down at his hands for a long time.

"No," his voice is so soft I almost miss it. "I won't make you go anywhere, but I can't leave you. If there's somewhere you want to run to, let me run with you."

After first I felt a jolt of fear when he said no, but his explanation catches me even more off guard. It's more emotional than I was expecting from him.

"I owe them, but they don't own me, Aspen. I won't force you to them. Even if I think it'll be good for all of you to meet and clear the air, if you're not ready it will do more harm than good." He takes a deep breath and pulls back onto the road. "I'm here for you. If finding somewhere to hide you and keeping it from them is what we need to do, I'll do it. If I need to let you go on your own, if that was the best move, I'd fucking try. If taking you to a place I know is safe and protected by men and women I trust, if I can do that without putting you or them in more danger, than that's what we'll do. Do you understand?"

"Yes." I swallow. "I wondered if it was a setup." Might as well be honest with him since the thought is still going to circle in the drainpipe of my brain and it will fuck with me more than just this once. It's giving him fair warning that I might panic again.

"The men at your cabin?"

"Yes."

"Fuck." Gailen shakes his head and looks genuinely hurt. "Let's not pretend you haven't snooped into every aspect of my life. Does that really seem like something I would do?"

"It doesn't. However, I have never claimed to be sane or rational."

He grunts. "You're both. Probably more rational than is healthy, which is why you had that thought. Are we good? Do you still trust me?"

I reach out and put my hand over his where it rests on the steering wheel.

"I still do."

Gailen puts his other hand over mine and squeezes lightly. We sit there like that, some kind of comfort feedback loop, caught up in the reality of touching each other. I feel the heat of his hand all the way up my arm. It's incredible. Touch has never been important to me, other than touching Troy.

He comforts me and distracts me when I play with his fur, but for me it's always been other things that my dog gave me that centered me. His brown eyes, his pink tongue. The consistent smell of his doggy breath and his musky fur. The realness of his breathing, his sniffling, and hearing him slop up water from the bowl. I do love digging my hands into him. Scratching his ears and watching his happiness at getting attention. I thought it was just how it was with dogs, that touch wasn't a sense that was heightened for me.

I'm wrong.

Touching Gailen heightens everything, including my other senses. He smells sharply of citrus, like fresh oranges. It amuses me because my favorite scent is grapefruit - it's my shampoo, body wash, and lotion. We're complimentary there. I can hear his steady breathing in the dark of the car, and I can't seem to look away from where his hand holds mine. The veins on the back, his defined knuckles, his almost brutally short fingernails.

My heart is racing again.

I extricate my hand but shift so I'm closer to him in my seat. Close enough that his body heat is detectable across the console. Everything in my world has turned upside down in a day and I'd be stupid to keep myself from the comfort his existence gives me. I'll figure this situation out, I always do, but for the first time I might not have to figure it all out alone.

16

Gailen

At some point I feel in my gut that we're far enough away from danger for the moment. I pull off at the first roadside motel I find, and breathe a sigh of relief there aren't any cameras. Aspen doesn't even question me when I obscure the license plates to make it harder to find us. We need to rest and regroup, and then we need to get a little further before we steal a car.

I don't know who these people are or what they could be tracking. It might be Aspen, but I'd bet they'd have an easier time tracking me if they know who I am. I haven't been actively trying to hide myself for years.

The clerk at the desk doesn't even look at me for longer than a few seconds when he takes my information, and doesn't blink at the fact that I'm paying in cash. If whoever is following us does find their way here, this man won't have anything to tell them.

Despite the dingy appearance of the outside, the motel room is nice. Everything is clean, the paint is fresh, and even if it's a little dated whoever takes care of this place takes care of it well.

While I send a few texts to check in and so Aster has our location, Aspen dips into the bathroom. Troy hops up on the bed and resumes sleeping. I can hear the shower running and don't let myself think about her naked.

When she comes out, her hair is up in a messy bun and she's wearing leggings instead of the shorts we ran out in. The over-sized sweatshirt she's drowning in makes me want to cuddle her into my arms. I want to figure out what cozy feels like with her. It's never something that appealed to me before.

I've always wanted to be on the move. For Aspen, I want to figure out how to be still.

When I realize that I've been staring, I clear my throat and move past her to use the bathroom myself.

Before leaving it, I meet my own eyes and remind myself that we're in danger. I need to be careful, and I need to be smart. Aspen is a temptation I never planned on and need to tread carefully around. I'm not going to lie to myself that I can keep away from her, or avoid the obvious pull between us. She's determined and crafty; Aspen will pursue this and we can't be at odds with each other if I plan to keep her protected.

I won't pretend like I don't want to peel her out of that sweatshirt and explore her body with my tongue, but there are going to be boundaries. The intensity of the situation magnifies the intensity of our feelings, and I have to be cognizant of that. I can't let the situation rush us.

One careful, savoring, step at a time.

I'm never leaving her, so there's no reason to hurry.

I'm hers in whatever capacity she'll have me.

Aspen is already in bed when I leave the bathroom. I plug in my charger and then my phone, turning on the sound so any notifications or calls will wake me up. She rolls over before I can get in next to her. Her face is pale and drawn, so I move over to her side and kneel down next to her.

Without thinking about it, I brush her hair out of her face, and she gasps sharply.

"What's wrong?"

"I was done running, and now I'm running again." Her eyes are so sad.

"You were running away. We're running towards something this time."

Aspen sits up and puts her feet on the ground, then her face in her hands. "If you say so."

I move to kneel next to her, and should probably back away.

The warmth of her body sinks into me and I feel like I'm breathing again, like I did when we were holding onto each other in the car. Memories of this strange, scattered night come back to me.

"Why were you coming downstairs?" I ask.

"What?" She looks up and her cheeks turn pink.

"Why were you coming downstairs when I came to get you?"

The pink tinge darkens. "I was coming to you."

My body tightens. "Why?"

Aspen looks away and bites her lip, but then she answers. "I want you."

I didn't expect her to be that direct. It makes me hard in a second, and I stare at her furiously blushing face until she turns to meet my eyes. The heat in her gaze makes my cock throb, but I swallow down my desire and try to hang onto my control.

"We shouldn't."

"That's not the same as not wanting to, Gailen." There's surprise and intrigue in her voice. As if she was unaware of how much I want her.

"We barely know each other, emotions are heightened, and we - who we are to each other - that's fucking complicated. You're 19."

"Pfft," she scoffs. "I've never been a kid, and you know that better than anyone. I'm not innocent or naive."

"I won't take advantage."

Aspen laughs, that rusty, raspy sound that hits me center mass. "Like you could."

We stare at each other.

"I know myself. I know what I want, and I know how I feel. Do you want me?"

For the first time, I'm the one that looks away. Aspen shifts so that I'm now kneeling between her legs. Not close enough that we're touching, but close enough to be tempting.

"Look at me, please."

I can't disobey the sweetness in her request.

"Of course I do," I finally answer her question. "Since I stood in your hallway and watched you sleep."

One side of her mouth lifts in a smile, but her expression is serious. "Then why not?"

I shake my head, trying to cling to the boundaries that need to exist between us.

"If I kiss you, will you let it go for tonight?"

Now she grins. "Yes."

"Promise?"

"Promise."

I shift forward so my torso is touching her knees, then her thighs. My hands reach up to dive into her hair and cradle her head, pulling her toward me. Aspen's eyes flutter shut and I'm amazed and honored that she's so immediately vulnerable with me. I feel in this moment how much she trusts me. Aspen's hands rest softly on my waist but she might as well be gripping me hard from the intense feelings that touch gives me.

Our mouths meet and press, and I suck her bottom lip between mine. She gasps and presses harder into me, her tongue teasing my lip and requesting entrance. I didn't want to go deeper but I can't help it. My jaw relaxes and I dip my tongue in to dance with hers, tasting Aspen.

Her lips turn up in a smile I can feel, and we move against one another with only our mouths.

I break the kiss but don't pull away. It takes a long moment for her to open her eyes and meet mine.

"Go to sleep."

"Okay."

"Don't grope me in the middle of the night."

Aspen smiles slowly. "Okay."

We get into the bed and turn off the lights.

Both of us lay still, but I can tell neither of us is drifting off to sleep.

"You said in the car that I looked into you…which is true." Aspen lets that linger. I have a feeling I know what she's going to ask me, but it's not something I'm going to offer up freely.

"You disappeared for 3 years. I know a very well disguised shell company paid you, but I could never find out what you did. That's the mystery of you, Gailen," she says softly, and once again my body reacts to her saying my name.

"Is there a question in there?" I offer. I don't want to explain, but I will if she wants to know.

"Where were you?"

I sigh and turn over onto my back to stare at the dark ceiling.

"I was a mercenary."

Silence.

"Like the guys who came to my house?"

"Something like that. They trained me, sent me to do jobs, and paid me well. It's the reason Alina hired me. It's how I was able to track you."

"Have you killed people?"

"Yeah, Aspen. I think that's a given."

"Do you regret it?" There's genuine curiosity and not judgment in her tone, but I'm still glad that I can't see her face right now. If she was disgusted or appalled, I don't think I could handle it, not now. Not after kissing her.

"My team specialized in kidnapping extraction, but some of my ops had collateral damage. I don't regret the people I saved, but what I did wasn't without consequences. I feel them."

"That makes sense. But why…" she trails off but I can hear her thinking. "Why do you keep that a secret?"

"One, to keep the organization safe. I left, but they're still going. Second, I lost friends. I saw people I felt bonded with get hurt, or die. It's not a highlight in my life. It was a step I took because I thought it was necessary for my survival."

"Do you still think that?"

"I think I grew up in a life that made me want to be dangerous. Dangerous enough that no one would ever mess with me." Growing up, I was neglected by my parents who had their own burdens, and regularly bullied. There's no doubt in my mind that Aspen knows about the broken arm, black eyes, and fights once I started high school.

I hear Aspen shuffle on the bed and can see the outline of her change as she turns to face me.

"You're plenty dangerous, Mr. Burke." The amusement in her voice relaxes me.

"Get some sleep, Aspen."

She lets out a huff of a laugh, and silence falls over us again.

17

Aspen

If he hadn't told me explicitly not to grope him, I probably would have tried. I'm definitely going to think about it. Gailen has given me a lot to think about tonight. More than I expected, but a nice distraction from the crisis that's cracking my heart.

It's not like I've kissed hundreds of people, but I think I can definitively say that was the best kiss of my life. The best kiss of anyone's life. Feeling him weaken and break and kiss me deeper sent a shiver of power through my body. It destroyed the last speck of hesitation I had that he didn't want me in return. Gailen is as caught up in this unexpected feeling as I am, and the more we give in to it the better it feels.

Part of me wonders if we hadn't been attacked, how long would it have taken us to break down the wall? How long would fear have kept space between us? Right now we're both worried about surviving, as we should be, but when this is settled and we have to talk about the reality of our feelings it's going to be a mutually enlightening conversation.

Gailen is the man of my literal dreams and nightmares.

For the last four years, I've seen him in my sleep almost every night.

Sometimes good, sometimes bad. Sometimes I fight him because I'm back in the guilt and the darkness and I want to die; in the worst ones we die together. Other times, it's the relief I felt when he picked me up and carried me out because I couldn't walk. I don't fight him, I burrow into him, cling to the safety of him.

Is the smoky scent I associate with him real, or is my mind that powerful? I can still smell the smoke. On the bad days I still feel the burn, and my arm tingles and stretches in a way that I hate. I can't imagine how bad it must get for him. To be honest, I haven't had the guts to ask him about his injuries. I haven't wanted to talk about mine.

I feel like he'd push back at me to protect himself. My gut tells me there will be a time when we clear the air of the past, including how it's impacting us in the present.

Still, why him? Why of all people in the world is he the one that makes every one of my senses come alive? I might as well have been sleeping through the last few years given how awake I feel now. Not awake in the sense of not tired, but alert in a way I didn't know had been missing.

Awareness. That's what it is. Of my body, my inner self, my mind, my needs.

He doesn't make me anxious or nervous, not all the time anyway, he soothes me. It's like everything is clear now.

I want him. Not just physically, although damn he is pretty and I want him that way. On an emotional and mental level, I want to dig into him and pull him into me. I want to be so enmeshed in each other on every level that we can never be untangled. I've been running from him until I was ready for him, and whatever happens, I'm going to fight for him in the end.

The violence I know he's capable of should scare me, but I find myself intrigued. It gives me confidence that we'll survive this.

I fade off to sleep thinking about his hands on me and the taste of his mouth.

When I wake up the next morning, Gailen is already dressed and alert. He's on his phone, and I take a moment to watch him and enjoy looking. His body is slouched in the chair, his legs out and spread open, a stance that appears relaxed but I can see the tension. Gailen runs a hand through his damp hair and then his golden eyes lift up to meet mine.

There's a hint of a smile before he schools his expression. He's happy to see me.

"We should get on the road."

I nod and get up, stretching like usual. We slept in the same bed last night but I have no memory of being beside him other than our little chat. That's disappointing. He definitely slept there because when I look over there's a dent in the pillow and the sheets are rumpled. Part of me thought he'd chicken out and leave after I fell asleep.

It's unusual that I would sleep that deeply, but it's probably another thing that's because of him. There's no need to be on guard when he's guarding me instead.

My morning routine is quick and I dress comfy because we're either going to be in a car or running. Despite the stress, I look happy when I see myself in the mirror. I look relaxed. There aren't even dark circles under my eyes. His presence is that powerful.

Gailen packs the car as I take Troy to do his business and clean up after him. I tease him a little bit with a chew rope to get some of his energy out, and he prances around me and plays. When I look over, Gailen is leaning against the Land Rover, muscly arms crossed, watching us with something close to the expression that was on my face in the mirror. Contentment.

I tap my thigh and Troy follows me. We wait in the car while Gailen checks us out of the motel.

We start driving, and there's a comfortable silence between us. It feels like we've done this a hundred times. Like we always take road trips together. I wish.

"Listen," Gailen starts, but he stops when I sigh. "What?"

"This is about them, isn't it?" My stomach pits, but I try to make myself hear him out.

He nods. "I'm not saying we have to go there, or that you have to jump headfirst into things with them, but could you at least call? Open a line of communication."

"Why?" I'm genuinely asking why he thinks that's a good idea, not with sarcasm, and when he glances at me quickly he sees that.

"So you can make an informed decision, and I think because you know there are some amends to make."

Shame flashes hot in my chest.

"A lot has changed about all of you in four years."

"You're right. I'll give it a try." I mean it. I can't say that it's going to make a difference in the long run, but it's definitely a form of closure. For all of us.

"That's all I'm asking. Thank you."

I shift in the seat so I'm facing him. "You're really doing all of this out of guilt? Because you think you owe them?" It's a harsh question and maybe I shouldn't have asked it so bluntly. Then again, if Gailen hasn't both realized and accepted my bluntness by now, this will never work.

Gailen tilts his head, thinking before he answers. I like that about him.

"It started that way. I take pride in my work, and I failed both them and myself. I had something to make up to them, and something to prove to myself. When it comes to you though…"

I wait, but he doesn't continue.

"It's complicated."

I smirk at his answer, but leave it at that. Damn right it's complicated.

I don't think I'd want to be anything less.

18

Aspen

"Where are we going?" I finally crack, since he seems to be following GPS directions to somewhere in particular and it's been a few hours already.

"We rented a cabin under a fake name. It should be isolated enough that your car won't be spotted until we can get a new one, but defensible. Harp found it."

That doesn't really mean anything to me in terms of decision-making but if it makes Gailen feel reassured then I'll go with it. While I did play board games with the silent, deadly giant those years ago in the hospital, he wasn't the easiest person to read. The only thing about him that was obvious besides his silence was his devotion to Aro. I'd never seen a man look at a woman that way; not even when Owen looked at Anora.

I don't think I believed love existed until I saw the way my sisters and their men interacted. The instinctive understanding and support of their partner was obvious. The fact that all these people lived together most of the time and seemed to genuinely like each other was shocking. They loved each other as family, friends, and lovers, and they didn't downplay their emotions.

That was a kind of freedom I'm not sure I'd ever experience. All the therapy in the world couldn't undo the training I'd had since birth to hide what I was feeling as much as possible. Gailen brought it out of me sometimes, but I don't think I would ever be in a place to be that vulnerable with the Sorrelles. My fear of them hurting me would always win.

"It'll give us a chance to research and make a plan. We won't know what the next best move is until we know who we're fighting." Gailen continues, explaining why we're doing what we're doing.

"We?"

"Fuck off," he snaps back with no heat, knowing that I'm messing with him. I feel oddly relieved that I'm not alone in this. Not just having Gailen, but having the Sorrelles at my back. It's selfish of me to take advantage of their care and generosity, but I also want to live, and this is the best way to do that.

"Have you pissed anyone off extra special lately?"

"That's a long list, but most of them would blame the collective, and have no idea about us individually." I've been racking my brain since we left to try and figure it out.

Gailen nods, and we don't say anything as he drives for awhile. We're in a woody area and must be getting closer to the cabin because we're making more turns and slowing down. It's gorgeous, and makes me miss my home.

The cabin is in a little clearing in the woods and it's very simple. There's a concrete porch in the front with two nice deck chairs and a little table, but otherwise the place is a plain wood rectangle.

I follow Gailen inside and it's cozy. A living area in the front that includes the kitchen, doors into two bedrooms, and a third door into the bathroom. Basic but comfy. I glance down at the laminated welcome letter on the table by the front door. It's got wi-fi. That's all I care about.

Gailen puts his bag in one room, and mine in the other.

I smile to myself if he thinks that's going to last. We're out in the middle of nowhere with only each other and very few distractions. We're doing pretty good at fighting the tension, but we're not that strong. This force pulling us together will likely overpower our resistance.

"Can I trust you to behave if I leave you alone?" Gailen asks, toying with the keys to the Land Rover. "I need to go get supplies."

"Where am I going to go?"

He rolls his eyes. "That's not an answer."

I wait until he's looking at me. "I'm not leaving you."

Gailen's expression softens. "Any requests? Anything you need?"

"Food for Troy," I start, and my dog perks up his head from where he was sleeping on the overstuffed love seat. I mention a few other snacks, but otherwise everything else I need for a solid week is in my go bag.

Before he leaves, Gailen steps close to me and takes my hand. "If anyone comes, you run. Don't wait for me, don't hide, run. I'll find you."

"Maybe." I stand on my toes and kiss his cheek, lingering there and enjoying the sharp citrus scent and the undercurrent of smoke. He smells like strength and safety. Part of me misses him already, feeling empty to know that he'll be away from me.

It's insane, but it's true.

Gailen's hand wraps around my waist and he squeezes once before stepping back and leaving the cabin. I watch through the screen door until he's gone.

Then I flop down on the love seat next to Troy and make the easiest of the calls I promised Gailen I would make. There's no time like the present to get things done. If I start procrastinating it, I'll never stop.

She doesn't answer, so I leave a voicemail. Once she knows it's me,

I know she'll call. I wouldn't answer an unknown number either. It only takes a few minutes before my phone is buzzing. I dig my fingers into Troy's neck scruff and answer the call.

"Hey."

"Hey yourself," Aster drawls. "What's up?" Like we talk all the time. Like this is just a regular phone call.

"I…" I have no idea what to say.

"Let's talk business first, and then try the rest, yeah?"

"Yeah." Computer skills aside, Aster and I are the most alike. We are blunt, cagey with our emotions, easily frustrated, and unafraid of being obviously other. I think I'm gentler than her, but no less protective of myself. I pull my laptop out of my bag, get on the cabin wi-fi, and open up my files.

"Send me a link," I tell her and rattle off one of my encrypted email addresses. In a few minutes there's a secure link to a drive on her server, and I upload files for cases that I took on myself, which includes everything from my uncle to minor celebrities to politicians. Those are the only case that make me vulnerable. They were things I did outside the collective for various reasons. None of them were paid, all of them were personal on some level.

"Everything I've done on my own."

I hear Aster clicking and scrolling on the other side of the call, and then her huff of a laugh. "Been busy, hm?"

"The world won't save itself," I say to the woman who kills abusers as a hobby.

"It doesn't know how. This gives Isaac and I some good starting points. We have a friend or two we might bring in, are you okay with that?"

"About this, yes."

Silence falls between us as she works, and it's oddly comfortable to listen to her type and click and work. To know that she's doing work to help me, and to figure out who wants to kidnap me. I didn't think I'd like the way that felt; to be helped by them. I didn't think I'd earned it, but if anyone would do this for fun and not because of who it was, it's Aster. She'd do this to stick it to a jerk, so I'm not sure how much of this is about me at all. Some of the anxiety leaves me at that thought, and makes me let go of the idea that I'll owe her for this.

"I would have run too, you know."

It comes out of nowhere and it takes me a minute to respond. "Really?"

"Yeah. If I had been in your situation, after being so controlled for so long, I would've chosen chaotic freedom. We would never hurt you, but we can be smothering and you didn't need that, even when it came from a good place."

"I didn't. But I don't know if I did the right thing either."

"You let us know you were alive. I won't lie, you broke some hearts, but not in ways that can't be healed. They don't understand what you went through. Hell, I barely understand and I'm the poster child for how trauma can warp you. So from one runner to another, I get it, and I'm not mad at you."

"I'm still sorry. I hope I didn't seem ungrateful."

"There's nothing to be sorry for, nothing to forgive. But this is probably your last second chance, so don't fuck it up."

"Got it." I want to laugh because she's trying to be dry, but I can't. I can't because I know it's my last chance to figure things out with them. I refuse to keep breaking their hearts because I can't figure my shit out and find a way to view "family" as anything other than the enemy. I need to believe that they won't try to control me and turn me into something that suits their view like Elton did. All of them are so different, and they disagree with each other, but the love is still there. I could be part of that, within reason.

It's not even like this because Elton tried to indoctrinate me into believing the Sorrelles are the enemy, but because the way he treated me and mom made me believe family can't be trusted. Even if they show themselves to you as good and loving people, someday their selfishness and inner darkness will win. Someday they'll throw you down and hurt you, and not care that they did it if they get what they want in the end.

That's my real fear.

"Take your time. I'll look into this stuff and keep you guys in the loop. Is Gailen there?"

"Supply run."

"I'll text him."

Silence again.

"If you ever need to talk, I'm here. Or if you need someone to be on the other end of the line, just existing, I can do that too."

"Thanks. Same."

Aster laughs and hangs up the call. I knew she'd be the easiest, and everything else from here is an uphill climb. I lay down on the love seat and wait for Gailen to get back.

Even though that went well, I can't stop the tightness in my chest or the feelings that are overwhelming me. I'm not going to cry, and even if I did I don't know if I'm crying happy or sad tears. I don't know what this feeling is, I just know I feel like a strong breeze could shatter me.

19

Gailen

Something is off with Aspen when I get back, but I give her space. Aster texted me that they talked, so I assume she's processing that conversation. Part of me feels bad that when it comes to them she doesn't really have privacy. We're all going to swap information trying to take care of her. While I've started to back off on that, it comes from a place of fear of losing her.

Aspen's head is tilted toward her laptop screen but her eyes are unfocused, and she's petting Troy. The dog has his head on her hip and keeps looking up at her, monitoring that she's okay. Same dog, same.

I put away the groceries and supplies that I picked up - enough to last us at least a week - and go about checking the security of the cabin. Both bedrooms have a large, unscreened window, so we have a back egress if we need it. Even the window in the bathroom is big enough that we could sneak out if needed. It's got a huge, old cast iron bathtub so there's also a safe place to get cover from bullets.

After stomping around for a bit, which Aspen doesn't even react to, I find the door for the cellar. She turns to watch me go down to the small empty space, but still doesn't say a word. Troy hops off the couch to sniff at the open door in the floor, then resumes his vigil with her.

"Want to go for a walk?" I ask.

"Yeah, that might be good." I feel relieved when she answers, and wait for her as she puts a lead on Troy.

As we start to follow the trail behind the cabin, I reach out my hand to her. I'm not going to be hurt if she rejects it but I feel like she needs me right now. Aspen will talk when she's ready, but I need to remind her that I'm here.

Her small hand slides into mine and she weaves our fingers together. It fits in a way I don't expect but I should have. I don't think I've held hands with anyone like this since high school. The sweetness of it feels good. She hasn't had enough sweet.

Troy sniffs at everything and pees on a bunch of trees, so we keep our pace slow. The sun is filtering through the leaves and the air is warm and moist. It's much better here than in the city, that's for sure. I can breathe deep and only get the rich scents of earth and greenery. It's got nothing on how good Aspen smells, but I'll take it.

We find another small clearing and Aspen lets go of Troy's leash so he can run around and sniff. She stops in the middle and turns her face to the sky. Aspen takes big, deep breaths, in through her nose and out through her mouth. She's still holding my hand and instead of looking up, I'm looking at her.

There are honey colored streaks in her dark brown hair. With her face tilted up I can see that she had her nose pierced at some point but let it close. There are scars along her jawline, her eyebrow, and I want to touch them with my lips and tongue. I want to soothe every hurt, even if it's physically healed. I want her to know every mark makes her even more precious to me.

"It's nice out here," I tell her. She takes a deep breath and I watch her chest rise.

"It is. I don't think I'm made for city living." Aspen finally looks down and our eyes meet. "You a city boy, Gailen?"

"I was, and then I wasn't." It's cryptic, but I think there are parts of myself I'm not ready to reveal to Aspen yet. She might know about my missing years as a mercenary, but I didn't let her in how much those years bent and broke me. How much I needed an escape after leaving my team. I loved Chicago, it's where I come from, but the isolation of the Sorrelle compound was restorative for me. It was open and green, and I wasn't oppressed by the feeling of eyes everywhere. I was the eyes.

We'll talk about it. I know she'll bring it up again when her mind circles back around to it.

Aspen's stomach audibly grumbles, and I give a small laugh before pulling her back toward the cabin. She calls for Troy and he dutifully trots up to her and follows us back, his lead dragging behind him. It's good to have in case we encounter a predator, but otherwise that dog isn't leaving Aspen's side.

Back at the cabin, I assure her that I'll cook and start making us an early dinner. I spent a lot of hours hanging out in the Sorrelle kitchen and it was hard not to pick up a few things or straight up ask to be taught.

Keeping in mind that Aspen is a vegetarian, I grabbed a good eggplant to make Parmesan. I start pulling together ingredients and making it, along with some noodles. While I would prefer chicken, the eggplant will do. It's easier to cook for both of us than try and make separate things.

The scent of the food quickly fills the cabin and it draws Aspen over to the kitchen area like a cartoon mouse smelling cheese. She sits on a stool at the counter and watches as I make some garlic bread too, and throw that in to the oven to bake.

"If you were trying to get me to not want tear your clothes off and jump on you, this isn't how you do it." Her tone is dry and it reminds me of Aster. I give her a small smile but don't comment. It's hard enough to keep my dick under control.

"I mean you're a badass and all muscly, you can cook, and you're pretty. What else am I supposed to do?"

Now I stop. "I'm pretty?"

"Yeah, you're pretty." She props her elbows up on the counter and puts her chin in her hands, then exaggeratedly looks me up and down. "So pretty."

There are so many things I want to say in reply to that, and none of them are appropriate. I just shake my head and keep working, even while I feel her eyes on me with so much power she might as well be touching me. I'm rock fucking hard now, and I know she can see it, but I say nothing.

I plate a serving for each of us as well as noodles and garlic bread.

We eat in silence, although Aspen moaned when she took her first bite and that was pure evil. She fidgets a lot, her leg shaking back and forth, causing her knee to hit my thigh every once and awhile. Each bump sends sparks through my body.

Somehow, we're more alone out here than we were at her house. Maybe it's that our trust has grown in the last day and a half, or the fact that there will only be a wall between us instead of a whole floor, but it's like every cell in my body is more attuned to her than ever.

Last night was torture. I slept above the covers on my back so that I would be ready to act at the slightest sound, but it also meant I could see her easily. The way her lips dropped open slightly, that sometimes she scrunched her nose in her sleep, and every rise and fall of her chest when she breathed. I learned every millimeter of her that I could see in great detail last night.

She staggers me.

I think I'm in love with her.

I say I think because I've never been in love, so I honestly don't know. All I know is that she has power over me no one else ever has. Aspen could ask me for anything and I would do it. I want to protect her as much as I want to ruin her for everyone but me. I want to do what's best for her and have her reconnect with her family, while also wanting to live in this cabin and have her all to myself for eternity.

But I need her to chose that, if it ever happens, or I'll be no better than her brother. As much as I feel the possessive, obsessive desire to hide her away and create a world of only the two of us, that's not who she needs me to be. That's not what she needs from us.

Aspen goes back to her computer when we're done eating because her and Aster are working through things right now trying to find our enemy. I keep an eye on her as I clean up.

The sun fades, and as soon as it gets dark, exhaustion hits me. I've been running on lust and adrenaline for days now and if I don't get real sleep it won't be good. We're safe enough where we are that I can let go a little.

I step into the bathroom and get ready to sleep.

Aspen is waiting near the bedroom doors when I come out.

"Don't stay up too late. Wake me up if you need me."

"You really aren't going to sleep with me?" She's trying so hard to sound unbothered that I know it bothers her. I can't tell if it's because she's horny or because she's afraid to be alone. I'll take both or either, honestly.

"No. I'm really not."

"So you don't want me?" Her voice is defeated. There are too many layers to this conversation, and I am too tired to parse them all out right now. We are not having sex. Flat out, full stop. I'm not ready for that with her. I'm not ready for what that will do to me when it comes to how I feel about her, and my already high protective instincts will go into overdrive.

I go to her, trying to gather my thoughts into something coherent.

"Aspen." I give in and take her face in my hands. "We are not running out of time, and I am not going to rush what's happening. Of course I want you. From the moment you opened your front door and I looked in your eyes, everything I saw there, you've owned me. I belong to you."

She keeps looking down, taking in what I've said, and then her dark eyes flash up to meet mine.

"Do I belong to you?"

"No," my answer is soft and quick. "You will never belong to anyone but yourself, and you shouldn't after all you've been through. You're yours, but I'm yours, too."

We don't move as I watch the tears well in her eyes but they don't spill over down her cheeks. I think she gets it now, and I think she knows that even if I'm keeping boundaries and distance between us that it's not rejection. It's caution.

Aspen pushes my hands away and steps closer so she can put her arms around my neck. The hug surprises me, but I hold her in return. Her heart thumps against my chest and I'm surprised by how much it's racing. How it matches my own. I feel so goddamn much right now and I don't know what to do with it. I don't know how to do this.

I spent the early part of my adult life with feelings for the worst possible person for me, making her into something she wasn't, and the rest of it so far has been spent chasing Aspen. She's all I know, and I have to do this the right way so that there's never even a chance that I hurt her.

I promise myself I will never be another person in her life that fails her.

Automatically, I turn into her and inhale the sharp grapefruit scent she favors, and let the closeness of her relax me. We can start simple and easy, like this. Comfort first, the rest later.

"I'm going to get some sleep," I whisper, then kiss the top of her head.

Aspen gives me a soft smile as she steps away. Her cheeks have a hint of pink, but things feel settled between us.

For now.

20

Aspen

I behave myself for a week.

Mostly because I'm busy looking through every detail on every person I've even marginally brushed up against in the digital world for the last 4 years. Even the others in the collective have no idea, and as far as we can all tell, no one's identity has been breached. Their anonymity is still intact.

Which makes it even clearer that this is about me and something I've done.

I have a suspicion, but I think if it's real it will be too much for me to handle and we don't have time for me to have a meltdown. There isn't time for the kind of guilty overwhelm that will come with that truth, if it is the source of the threat.

Gailen also spends time on his laptop but he's looking through records from Aster and spending a long time on a chat with Harp and Owen. Sometimes he even laughs when he talks to them, and I like knowing that he wasn't as isolated as I was during our game of cat and mouse.

The thing is…I'm out of distractions now.

There's only so many walks I can take or games of fetch I can play with Troy before my mind drifts back to the sexy man sitting at the small kitchen island. To the way his shirt clings to his muscles, the way his jeans and even his sweatpants have to stretch over his thick thighs. I've spent far too long staring at his ass while he cooks. I'm pretty sure I heard him jacking off in the shower because he's quieter than me.

I've seen the outline of his cock when he gets hard because he feels my eyes on him.

He knows it too, and those smirks are even more deadly because he doesn't acknowledge it otherwise. He doesn't acknowledge the tension between us at all now.

Plus, it's not like I can masturbate because we're literally never apart, and these walls are fucking thin.

I had to accept after a day that a man I really want to have sex with is going to hear me pee. I tried getting off in the shower but one muffled moan and he was panicking that something had happened to me, which meant trying to get off in bed was definitely out.

Luckily, he did not figure out what I was up to, and I lied that I had a charlie horse in my calf. That was embarrassing.

Gailen is not what I expected. When we're not working, he tells me stories about growing up, more stories about the Sorrelles, and we have watched an ungodly amount of movies together in the last few days. It seemed easier than facing the tension of going to sleep in our separate beds.

I'm done with separate beds.

Gailen made lemon pepper fish and french fries for dinner, and it was light but filling at the same time. I let him think this is going to be a normal night. I do the dishes while he picks out a movie, and I sit next to him on the couch, close but not too close. I've been keeping some distance between us, but there's still far too many touches and casual brushes between the two of us for it to be an accident.

The kitchen is small but not so small he has to touch my lower back or put his hands on my hips every time he passes me. He doesn't need to touch me to get my attention when we're working in the same small space. There's no reason for him to hold my hand when we go out walking in the woods, but he takes it every single time, only letting go when we're playing with Troy.

I can't tell if he's doing it to drive me crazy, to reassure me, or maybe it's both.

Either way, this is my breaking point.

I took an intensive shower even after the water started to run cold, I'm wearing my favorite long tee, and comfy shorts with no panties. I'm not saying we have to have sex tonight, but I can't keep this flirtatious distance anymore when we both know this is something special, and it's going to be more. Yeah, we aren't in a rush, but there's also no reason to wait.

My heart almost fell out of my chest when he said he belonged to me. Gailen thinks I'm worth tying himself to, and I can't tell him not to bother because even if I don't think I'm worth it, I want him that badly. There's an energy inside me that wakes up when he's around, and I wish I could articulate what it was.

No one has ever understood my need to belong to myself. No one has ever seen me without me having to explain anything the way that he does. The audacity of that man understanding me so well when it's the last thing I was expecting.

He turns on a movie but I'm so focused on him that I don't even know what it is. I shift closer to him and lift my legs so they're resting against one of his. He stiffens beneath me but I see his nostrils flare.

"Gailen," I whisper, soft and needy. After a moment where he seems to be gathering his resolve, he turns to look at me. I reach for him, and run my fingers along the scruff on his cheek. His eyes close, and I feel the urge to run my lips over his long, dark eyelashes. I want to be the lashes that rest on his cheek. The teeth that bite into his lip. I want all of my skin touching all of his because I know that it's going to change everything for me.

For the first time, I might even be ready for it.

I don't let go of his cheek, but I shift and swing one of my legs over his, straddling him. Gailen groans and his hands fly to my hips, holding me back from snuggling my pussy right over his cock. A quick glance down and I can see he's already getting hard.

"I need you. Give me anything," I beg, "because I need to feel you."

Gailen's eyes open and meet mine, fierce and resistant.

I watch as the look softens in increments, and his arms relax. My hips slide up his thighs until I'm nestled against him, our cores pressing together.

"I need you to understand something," he starts, and my heart throbs at the sadness in his voice.

"I'm listening," I promise, focusing on what he needs to say and not how my body feels.

"I've been a second thought most of my life. Did you notice how none of my stories are really about me?"

I nod, and rest both my hands on his shoulders, squeezing lightly. I'm here, and I need him to feel it. I'm here for him and only him. He's being open with me right now in a way that I can tell hurts him, and I want to make that go away.

"I have never been anyone's first choice or priority. I've worked hard to be useful and have a purpose, but I have been, at best, a bit player in more important stories."

"So what? You're saying that you're only a guest star in mine?" The idea causes both pain and fear. Gailen isn't temporary for me.

A corner of his mouth kicks up. "No. What I'm trying to tell you is that if we cross this line, I will never let you go. When I said I belonged to you, I mean that I will live and die by your side, even when the moment comes you don't want me this way anymore."

I try to protest but he stops me with a shake of his head.

"We've been through too much to be optimists, Aspen." Gailen raises an eyebrow and I shrug because I can't disagree. Life hasn't exactly shown me that relationships are a good thing, let alone something that lasts, but I want him to be wrong. I'm choosing to be an optimist about us. If there's one trait I want to take from the Sorrelle side, its finding and believing in true fucking love.

"We're going to agree to disagree on this one," I reply. "Because if you belong to me, then I'm going to keep you, Gailen Burke. You are my first choice."

Before I can say anything else, or even see his reaction, Gailen yanks me forward and takes my mouth with his. The desperation in his kiss tells me everything that I need to know. I hold him to me, my arms wrapped tight around him as if I can force our cells to merge and we can physically occupy the same space.

His hands dive under my shirt and goosebumps follow as he traces my skin. I don't protest when he moves to take it off, leaving me in a plain, cotton bra. For a moment I tense when his fingers trail down my arm, and slow over the burn scar that goes from mid-bicep, over the point of my elbow, and an inch or so down my forearm.

Gailen breaks our kiss, still touching the slightly raised and hairless skin. It's faded with time, less angry and red, but it will probably be visible until my skin is too wrinkled too differentiate between burn and age. He doesn't look at it, only at me.

"I don't mind," I reassure him, and remove my bra before pressing my mouth back to his. Gailen slides his hands up to cup my breasts and I moan into his mouth when he lightly pinches my nipples. Lightning flashes into my core and my hips jump in a needy spasm. Our tongues tangle and tease, and I'm soaked already.

It feels good to touch him wherever and however I want when I've been so careful. Absorbing the feeling of his muscles, the heat of his skin, learning the touches that cause him to react. When I kiss along his jaw and lightly bite his ear he thrusts up, pressing into me and trying to hold in a groan. I keep teasing his ear with my tongue as I tease the waistband of his pants with my fingers.

"Can I touch you?" I ask, breathless and excited.

"Please," he groans and shifts so that I can undo his button and fly to get to him. Gailen's cock is hot and hard, and so thick I'm excited to feel him inside me. I'm going to be so full it'll border on pain and I want it. I want to be so focused on the feeling of him spreading me open that nothing else exists.

I push away from him and slide to the floor, tugging his clothes off his hips and down his thighs. His cock springs up, and I move to take him in my mouth. Gailen slides his hand into my hair and pulls back slightly as if he's trying to stop me. As soon as I taste him on my tongue I moan, sliding down and taking him as deep as I can. I love the taste of his skin and he smells of sharp citrus and salt.

I haven't given many blow jobs, but my enthusiasm makes up for skill because I could do this for hours. He's so velvety smooth and stretches my mouth. I use my hand to stroke him as I suck, and I know I'm doing well when I taste the first salty drops of his pre-cum.

"I need you," Gailen groans.

I let him go and stand up. "I need you," I answer, and slide my shorts off. I'm standing naked in front of him and there's clear reverence in his eyes. He's caressing me with his gaze, appreciating my body. It only makes me more aroused.

Gailen shifts as I move to straddle him again. He takes his cock in hand and holds me back, sliding his head along my slit and covering himself in my need.

"Bare?"

"Bare." It's practically a demand from me. "It's been 2 years, and I'm protected."

"Aspen," he groans, and there's such worship in his tone. "I don't deserve this. You."

"You do," I say as I place my hand over his and start to slide the head of him inside me. We both let go and he goes deeper, but there's resistance because I'm tight and he's big. I shift up and slide down again, working him deeper inside my body with each thrust. It feels even better than I thought, the way I'm being pushed apart, my body adjusting over and over to take him deep until I am as filled as I have ever been in my life.

My hips jerk and slide as I start to fuck him, getting wetter with every stroke until Gailen is there, pressed into my cunt all the way to the hilt.

I take a breath and meet his eyes.

"Mine," I whisper against his mouth before I kiss him again and roll my hips. I'm not in a rush. I'm not even going to bother working toward an orgasm, although I have no doubt I'm going to cum from this. All I want is to savor every second of his body inside mine, of the press of our forms, the aches and needs that we are fulfilling in one another. The pure act of sex and passion is enough.

It's intense to keep my mouth on his, to share our air, as his hands dig into my skin and we move together and away, back and forth, never going far but far enough to give us the friction we need. It's unbelievably pleasurable.

I've had fun sex, and I thought I'd had good sex.

Nothing touches this. He's fucking my soul.

My hands dive under his shirt because I want to feel his skin on mine. I move it up his body and he lets me to a point, but then tightens his arms against his body so I can't remove it.

I pull back, flexing my pussy around him because I can't stop.

"What's the matter?"

"I don't take off my shirt."

It takes a second for the haze of lust to clear and for my brain to put together why. I take his hand and place it on my scar.

"Do you think I, of all people, would find it ugly? I know what it means better than anyone."

Gailen looks uncomfortable and distracts me by running his hands over my body and cupping my breasts again. I lean back and he obliges me by taking a nipple into his mouth and sucking deep. I shiver and flex on his cock, getting wet and weak as he taunts me with his teeth, lips, and tongue.

"Let me see you," I whimper.

"I don't want you to feel guilty," he murmurs into the valley between my breasts and he moves to suck on my other nipple.

"I got over my guilt a long time ago. Please. I want to feel myself against you. I want nothing between us."

"Fuck," he hisses, and I rock my hips, using my body and want for him as part of my persuasion. "Anything you want."

He leans back and removes his shirt.

21

Gailen

Aspen's eyes trail over my body, followed by her nimble little hands. Her nails tease through my chest hair and across my nipples, causing me to groan involuntarily. I didn't even know that's a part of my body that was sensitive until she touched me.

Aspen smirks and then leans forward to press my body to hers.

She sighs in complete contentment as our skin meets, and wraps her arms around my neck. We're pressed forehead to forehead.

"I'm going to touch you," she warns, and her hands start to drop down to my back. When she touches the scar that stretches from my shoulder blades to the middle of my back, the familiar electrical, crawling feeling goes through me, but I don't pull away from her.

Aspen tilts her head and kisses my neck, my jaw, teasing my ear more, as she feels the shape of the damage.

"My hero," she whispers into my throat. It makes my cock throb, to hear her say it in that worshipful, aroused voice. It's dripping like honey all over me. "No one has ever deserved me except you."

It sets me off in a way I didn't expect. I grab her ass and push off the couch, stepping out of my pants and boxers but keeping myself buried inside her. I walk us to the bedroom she's been sleeping in because it's closer, and I fall onto the bed with her.

One of my hands is cradling her head, the other has a tight grip on her ass, tilting her up toward me, and I roll my hips. Aspen cries out and I swallow it with a kiss. I fuck her slow and steady, drawing out my pleasure and hers, winding her up over and over but not letting her tip over the edge. I never want to leave this moment. I want the two of us to be so lost in each other that the world no longer exists.

I want to fuck her until we both die from dehydration and starvation. I don't need food, water, maybe not even air. Just her. Only her.

"Gailen, please," she begs. I start moving a little faster, and a little harder, and it takes only a few thrusts before her thighs and her pussy clamp down on me.

Aspen throws her head back and cries out, and I watch her let go, emotional walls fully dropped, as she comes around my cock. Her skin is flushed, her mouth is open and there's a hint of a smile, but it's her eyelashes fluttering against her cheeks that strikes me the most. It's enough to break me, and I feel my release barrel out of me. I groan, pounding her hard as I can't take my eyes off the expression on her face. I will do anything to keep that look of pleasure and relaxation, and whatever it takes to see it again and again.

I collapse over her, but she doesn't seem to mind because immediately she wraps her arms around me and presses tight. Like she's afraid I'll move away too soon.

Finally she double taps my back and I move up enough to slide out of her. She gives a little gasp, and I move to the side and flop down on my stomach. I keep my arm wrapped around her waist to keep her close.

Aspen squirms for a moment and then rolls onto her side. I hide my smile when she snuggles closer, lining the front of her body up with the side of mine. The unrestrained giggle she lets out when I move my arm down so I can palm her ass makes my heart flutter.

Softly, she traces the burn scar. It's ugly, red, massive, and will never truly heal. There's a weird smooth patch in the middle where they used a skin graft to heal the worst of it. The part that burned the deepest, far past the dermis. I'm lucky I didn't die of infection, which is the biggest danger for a burn victim.

It surprises me that I don't mind her touching it. I thought it would bother me more, her seeing it, knowing exactly how it came to be, but it's actually easier. Aspen knows what I did and why I did it. Before I might have felt differently, but now that I'm with her, it almost makes me proud. It's a scar I bear because I saved her. It's a mark of how much I would do for her, before I even knew her. There's no limit to the damage I would endure for her now.

"My hero," she whispers again, and kisses my shoulder. When she moves out from under me and straddles my legs again, I tense up, but I also feel like I need to let her do this. Aspen leans over my back and presses her lips to my spine, right between my shoulder blades, just where the scar starts.

I force myself to feel it as she kisses her way down, across the mangled landscape of my body, until she's at the unblemished skin of my lower back.

"Thank you," she says, and even though I feel her breath in one place on my skin it's like I feel it in every inch of my body.

Then I feel her teeth sink into my ass cheek and let out a very undignified yelp.

"Sorry," she laughs, not sorry at all. "Couldn't help it."

I roll over and yank her back to me, holding her close where she should be.

I wasn't exaggerating before I gave in to her - this changes things for me. Aspen has been my reason for existing for years because the hunt was all I had. Now she's my reason for *living*, and that's an entirely different motivation. I want to do more than exist, and I want to do it all with her.

First, I have to make sure that she's safe.

Then, it's whatever the hell we want.

22

Gailen

Aspen is still deeply asleep when I slide out of her bed the next morning to make breakfast. It's like the air changes when she wakes up because I know as soon as she does, and I know she's coming out of the room before I can hear or see her. When I look over, she's drowning in my shirt from yesterday and I love how it looks on her.

I'm trying to let go around her, so I'm only wearing sweatpants. I don't know the last time I walked around shirtless that wasn't getting in and out of the shower. My back is always covered. The number one priority for a long time was covering my scar, both for myself and for others. I didn't want to tell people about it and I didn't want them to feel compelled to ask.

For Aspen, I'll strip myself bare. Inside and out.

"Scrambled eggs or omelet?"

"Scrambled eggs," she answers, and sits at the small island in the kitchen to watch me cook. I don't feel self-conscious under her gaze and it's an odd experience. Being self-conscious and hyper-vigilant has been standard operating procedure for me for so long that the pure relaxation I feel in Aspen's presence is enough to get drunk on.

I'm sliding her a plate full of eggs sprinkled with cheese when my phone buzzes. It's Aster. She speaks before I can say a word.

"It's Roger Forrester."

"Fuck." I take the phone from my ear and put it on speaker. "Aspen's here."

"What did you do to Roger Forrester?" Aster asks her, a laugh in her voice. "Because he's pissed as hell and throwing money at anyone who even vaguely says they can get to you."

I look up at Aspen and she's blushing, and her eyes are darting everywhere except to mine. Based on that, I think she had a suspicion it was him but was hoping that it wasn't.

"Aspen?" I prompt.

"He helped my brother, and I needed him to feel the consequences of that. I...I was going to fuck with his money but there was nothing he cared about more than power. I may have...harmed his reputation."

"I never heard anything," Aster answers. "There was no scandal or court cases."

"I went quieter than that," Aspen fidgets. "I knew who was supporting him and I made it worth their while not to; I blackmailed and I paid. He lost all of his access. His political career was effectively dead."

Aster laughs over the phone. "I love it. Well, he figured out it was you so someone talked. Derick is going to love this."

"Why?" Aspen asks.

"He hates Roger Forrester but left it alone because we asked him to. Now we're giving him a reason to burn the man alive. No one fucks with our family."

"What do we know?" I interject. Aspen got even more fidgety when Aster made the comment about family, and I know we'll have to circle back to that conversation soon.

"Only that he's paid a few different groups to track her down. Isaac and I are going to get all up in their business and see what they know, but you should probably start heading our way. Sooner rather than later."

Aspen and I meet eyes and she looks nervous.

"We'll let you know soon."

There's a long silence. "Okay." Aster hangs up.

"So, you fucked over your uncle." I try to fight my smile. It's very amusing that of all the things she could've done on the run, revenge was at the top of the list. The same would've been true for me. Burn down the ones who tried to burn you.

"I did. It took me two years, but I did it."

I walk around the island and pull her stool away from it. Breakfast is later. She gasps when I pull her legs open and step between them, but laughs when I grab her ass and lift her into my arms.

"Such a devious creature," I murmur into her neck, teasing her with my teeth and tongue.

"Yes," she doesn't deny it, and arches her body so I can have more access to her throat.

"I think that deserves a reward."

I set her down on the bed and slide up the shirt she's in to expose her lower half as I drop to my knees. She isn't wearing anything underneath, and I can see that she's wet already.

Aspen sits up on her elbows to watch as I nuzzle and kiss the skin of her inner thighs, going from one leg to the other. I grin up at her when her hips shift, and the scent of her arousal starts to reach me. I slide my hands over her silky skin, then tease with my nails until I can feel goosebumps under my lips.

She collapses back on the bed and whimpers in frustration, but I take my time tasting her skin before getting close to her core.

I lick her first, sliding her apart with my tongue and letting her flavor drive me wild. Aspen gasps and shivers, and I tease her entrance, working her up but not giving in to what she wants.

"I thought this was supposed to be a reward?" she pants, tilting her hips up to meet me. I laugh and she moans, so I give her what she needs. I find her sensitive clit and swirl my tongue around it, then suck on it, back and forth until I find the rhythm and pressure that makes her writhe. Last night our mouths were too busy on each other for me to make her scream my name.

Aspen's hands dive into my hair and she tugs as she grinds herself on my face.

I swirl the point of my tongue around her and she cries out, her body bowing up as she starts to come.

"Gailen," she huffs out, and then says it three more times as her orgasm races through her. I smile but keep sucking and licking. I stop when she pulls my hair in earnest, and kiss along her thighs again. I don't want to stop touching and tasting her.

"I need you," she says, and holds her arms out to me.

In a weird way, it reminds me of our shared past.

In a room full of smoke, a girl telling me she didn't want my help, curled in on herself. Now, a woman openly reaching for me, and telling me she needs me. It almost makes my head spin.

Instead of drowning in it, I move over her body and let myself be cradled between her thighs. Aspen doesn't break eye contact as she reaches down to line my cock up with her soaked pussy. I push inside her and we keep looking, watching as we take each other.

23

Aspen

Over the years, I've spent hours watching Gailen.

Literal hours.

I would sit in front of my computer and spy on him when he was looking through whatever hiding place I had him running to, watching as he methodically searched through everything to see if I left a trace of myself behind.

I've stalked him. Followed his movements through cities, wherever I thought a camera would be or where I could get away with hiding one. Gailen was an object of obsession, even if I didn't understand that at the time. Even if I didn't understand the nature of my obsession. There was a compulsion inside me to watch him and know what he was doing whenever I could. He was like a ghost in my life; a presence I was always aware of and thinking about even when I couldn't see him.

I thought I knew his facial expressions. I thought I knew him because I'd watched him through a camera and dug into his life on paper. To me, he was serious, melancholy, maybe even bordering on broody. Gailen was a grumpy man. That seemed like a certainty.

I was so wrong.

I had been watching a man with no reason to be happy. Sure, he'd had a purpose, but that purpose had also been a self-imposed punishment. The more we talk and the more time we spend together, the more I see that lift away from him. Even though he is often serious, the brooding is gone. If anything, I feel like there's mischief now.

We're still on our opposite sides of the main room, but now when he catches me looking at him, he smiles. I've never been a smiley person but before I even register that I'm doing it, I smile back. Every single time.

We're happy.

It's the most bizarre thing.

My uncle is trying to have me captured or killed. I am on the run from the life that I built, moving toward the life that I ran away from, with the man who has been hunting me for 4 years.

And I am the happiest I've ever been in my life.

It's not like life has given me a lot of opportunities to be happy, but I know that I've never felt like this. I'm safe enough, I'm with someone I trust, and I like the way he treats me and the way I feel when I'm around him.

I never imagined wanting to be so domestic with anyone. Cooking, cleaning, going for walks, trusting someone else to take care of Troy... to take care of me.

My mother was broken and unable to fight for me. When I was little enough it was easy for her to keep me out of Elton's way. She could feed me and hide me and bear the brunt of his anger and instability. As I started getting more interested in computers and demonstrating prodigious skills, it pulled me away from her and into his orbit. I was a tool, not a human, not even a pet, and he often forgot that I required care.

Feeding, bathing, exercise, exposure. I was lucky mom tried hard to teach me about other things in life, to always point out to me that

Elton wasn't normal and he was wrong, even if we couldn't escape him. She made it clear we were captives, and that everything we did was done in order to survive. It was a pitiful way to live, but at least I'm alive.

Everything we did was at the mercy of Elton's whims and desires. What we ate, talked about, watched, listened to, and I never thought I'd want to share those decisions with anyone ever again. I never imagined I'd want to have a conversation about what to eat or take turns picking what to watch. I thought I needed control over every single thing in my life. I thought having that kind of control would keep me from being hurt or controlled

Turns out I just needed someone I could trust. Wholly.

We're happy, and that's shocking. We are happy in the face of chaos and danger, and I take that as a sign that it's real.

I walk over to where he's sitting and he turns to face me, already expressing concern. It's hard to keep the smile off my face when I wrap my arms around him and kiss him.

Gailen responds immediately and takes it deeper, sliding his tongue between my lips and teasing me. I sink into him and relish the feeling of him against me. He's solid and real, and he smells amazing. The second he's around me and his scent hits me, my entire body relaxes.

"What was that for?" he asks when I break the kiss.

"Because I can." I press a kiss to his nose and I'm surprised when he blushes a little at the silly moment of affection. It gives me hope that we'll figure out our version of a normal future together when all the madness is done.

24

Aspen

The reality that all of this danger is being instigated by Roger helps make it clear to me that the next Sorrelle sister I need to clear the air with is Alina. Next to me, her and her family are the ones in the most danger. Derick was not subtle about how much he hated Roger, and especially after they found he helped Elton, he publicly trashed the man.

Then I went and did my thing and made it even worse.

Even if Roger knows it was me, it doesn't mean he won't try to hurt them anyway. In my experience people have no qualms about using others as leverage. He would hurt them if he thought it would hurt me, of that I have no doubt.

It would hurt me, and not only because I'd blame myself. I don't want them to be hurt.

Gailen watches me pace from his perch in the kitchen.

"Just do it. The anticipation is going to make it worse."

"Alina is a protector. What I did put her family in danger when her whole life is built around keeping them safe. How can she ever forgive me for that?"

Gailen sighs and I stop to face him. "You don't want to hear the answer to that."

I put my hands on my hips and give him a look that clearly demands he tell me anyways.

"You're her family, too. Roger put you in danger, put all of them in danger, and you got back at him for that. That's how she's going to see it."

He was right, I didn't like that reasoning. Our relation by blood was not a good enough reason for them to excuse anything that I had done. We were nothing to each other. Well, Anora and I had a connection that I would not deny because we'd been through it together, but the rest of them...

That was a lie too. I'd been tied to Aster for years before I'd started attacking Designation. Watching what she did and how she did it, learning from the way she coded. We played a digital game together and even though I was a tool for Elton's motives, it had been fun to play with her. Every move and counter-move had taught me something. She'd been my teacher even when she didn't know it, and Aster and I understood each other. It was why calling her first had been so easy.

I didn't connect with Alina. We'd only ever spoken on the phone or in video calls. She was happy, despite what my brother had done to the Sorrelles, and that was what I cared about. I wanted them to be able to move on from his destruction.

"Give me." I hold my hand out for Gailen's phone. I didn't think Alina would answer a call from a number she didn't know, and I wasn't quite ready for any of them to have an easy way to contact me except Aster. My boundary, at least for right now, was that I reach out to them.

"Do you want me to go? Troy could use a walk." Our eyes meet and the tightness in my chest relaxes. He is the only person I trust with Troy, but I need the comfort of my dog for these conversations. Plus, Troy is already pressed up against me, aware of my stress, so he wouldn't leave even if I tried.

"I need to do this alone, but Troy needs to stay."

A small smile lifts Gailen's lips as he looks down to where my little mutt is desperately trying to comfort me.

"I'll wander. I'm a shout away." He slides off his seat at the island and prowls toward me. It takes a lot of will power to mentally keep myself present and not get lost in how much I want him. Gailen kisses me softly and I am so dazed I almost miss him walking out the door.

After a few fortifying breaths, I pull up Alina's number and hit call.

"What's up?" she answers, casually. I can hear a small voice chattering in the background. It makes me curious about her relationship with Gailen. We talked about her the least, and now I regret it.

"It's Aspen."

"Oh. Hi. Can you hold on a second?" There's some noises and muffled voices and I hear footsteps echo. She's going somewhere else to talk to me, and that feels like more consideration than I deserve. "Sorry, we were making a mess in the kitchen."

There's no tension in her voice at all. It knocks me off guard and now I don't know what to say or how to say it.

"I'm sorry," I blurt after too long of a silence.

"For what?" There's a hint of teasing now, and I have even less of an idea what to do with that.

"Stirring things up with Roger. I know he already hated Derick and then…"

"Before I say anything, can I ask you some questions?"

I move over to the sofa and sit down. "Yes." Troy jumps up next to me and rests his head on my knee. I focus on rubbing his soft ears and the little space between his eyes as I listen to her.

"Why did you run?"

The question that even Gailen hasn't asked directly yet, but his assumptions have been accurate. The rest of them have probably made a lot of assumptions, and most of them are probably right too, but there are so many layers to the decision that I made in that hospital room. I was young and broken, and I'd been alone so long that it was all I knew and what I thought I needed. If I wasn't going to be alone, I also wasn't going to be with them. I didn't deserve them.

"I'd spent my entire life being controlled; I needed to be on my own. I needed to figure out who I was without other people's expectations."

"We would have had those," Alina admits, still unruffled.

"I know."

"Were you ever going to come back?"

Part of me wants to say no, but if that was the case, I wouldn't be here right now. "Yes." I know that's true but I don't know how to explain it more than that.

"Okay. How did you protect yourself? You ran with nothing but a phone. What were you thinking?" Alina sounds both exasperated and curious. I like that she's asking reasonable, grounded questions. Not diving into my emotions, but into my thought process. Ever the strategist.

"I had somewhere to run to and I had a lot of resources. The hackers in my collective helped me, and I'd spent my whole life defending myself from a monster. I wasn't as vulnerable as you all thought I was. I'm still not."

"Hm," Alina grumbles on the other end. "That might be true. Okay."

"Okay what?"

"I'm not mad at you. I was, but I believe that you knew how to take care of yourself and that's all I needed to know. That you ran with a plan."

"I did."

"And Roger Forrester is not your fault. Even if you hadn't ruined him, which is hilarious, he would've found a reason to pick another fight with us. With Derick at least. We can take care of ourselves."

"Okay."

"But still, this is about our family so let's fight this as a family."

"I…I don't, um," I stammer. That's the crux of the issue. For them, family has always been their safe place. The thing that they could retreat to and rely on. For me, family was the enemy. My mom couldn't protect me and gave up eventually; Elton hurt me, used me, and abused me. Individually, I know the Sorrelles are trustworthy, but as a concept I struggle to put any faith in family.

"Ah," Alina answers. "That's it then. We're not your family."

"That's not it, not quite," I correct. "I just had a very different experience than you."

"When you get the chance, you should talk to the guys. Derick, Harp, Owen - they were all betrayed and hurt by their families. Even Isaac, to a degree. We made a family, we showed them that family could be a safe place. We can show you that, too."

"Gailen said the same."

"He's right. Think about it."

"I will. Um, thanks."

We awkwardly wrap up the call, and I imagine her going back to her kids and her husband, to the house in the woods that I have totally spied on. Two calls down, two to go. Now I have to ask myself what I want when it's over. Do I want to be a Sorrelle sister? Do I want to figure out what my place in that family looks like?

Despite the idea that Don Sorrelle rejected me being beaten into my head for years, I know that's not true. I believe Anora that he had no idea. By blood, we are family. They feel like they owe me something for not being there, but they don't. They didn't know I existed. The blood between us shouldn't matter.

I don't know yet if I want it to matter.

I end up falling asleep on the sofa with Troy as a blanket, Gailen's phone clutched in my hand.

The sound of the door opening has me sitting up and snapping to attention. Troy grumbles at me from his sleeping spot as Gailen steps toward me. He kneels down next to the sofa and slides an arm underneath me, pulling me close.

"You good?"

"Good." I arch my back and stretch and don't miss him looking at my body. "Save that look for later. Feed me."

Gailen laughs, and bringing it out of him makes me feel so damn good. I kiss his smile, and feel heat in my body as he lets it drop to kiss me back.

25

Gailen

The next morning, I'm tangled up with Aspen in her bed when my phone buzzing wakes me up. It's amazing how quickly I adjusted to sleeping with another person, but I like knowing that she's there. That I only have to turn to her and I can protect or hold her. That the few nights when she's struggled to sleep or had a nightmare, I'm there to calm her down.

Feeling her breath slow as she lulls back into sleep, and knowing that I did that for her, is a powerful rush. The way I make her feel safe and relaxed is grace I don't deserve, but I'm not going to fight it. She knows her feelings and I've never been less than honest with her.

I slide out from under her and take the phone from the charger before leaving the bedroom.

"Hey, kid," I answer by habit.

"I am nearly 30. I *have* a kid, I am not *a* kid," but Aro laughs because she doesn't really care. We were in the same grade although we didn't go to the same school, but there's something about Aro that's always innocent. I've called her kid for as long as I've worked for her family. It still fits.

"What's going on?"

"I think you should come to us. We're isolated, we're fortified, and honestly, if we have to circle the wagons it's safer for us to travel together."

"Yeah. We can do that." Aro isn't wrong that we need more people physically present and on our side. It's been too damn quiet and we're well hidden, but not that well. It makes me believe whoever is out to get her is regrouping and making a plan. My biggest fear is that they've stopped underestimating Aspen and they're going to come back with more firepower.

I can handle a lot, but I already know I'd risk everything to keep her safe or get her away, and I don't want to be another person that she loses.

"I'll have Harp come meet you, bring you in. He'll drop coordinates, then you can give him an ETA."

"So official these days. Is this how you talk when you're planning a hit?" I tease.

"Yes," she snorts at me. "And sometimes it's foreplay."

"I did not need to know that." We laugh together, and my chest loosens. After she got sober, Aro and I got a lot closer. I would never have held it against her for blaming me for what happened to Don and to her, but she did forgive me eventually. Of all the Sorrelles, I talk to her and Owen the most. I wouldn't call Owen my friend, and I think Aro wouldn't let me call her anything less.

With everything she'd been through, Aro was the most concerned about what my self-inflicted punishments might look like. She was afraid that I'd turn to substances, though I was never even tempted. I wanted redemption more than I wanted punishment. It still surprises me that they all forgave me, or that some of them never blamed me at all.

Aro feels like she's my own sister sometimes; the closest I've ever had to that kind of feeling. None of them should give me the time of day and yet here I am, joking around with the woman who got hurt because I wasn't where I should have been.

She and Harp like to remind me that if I had been there, I'd probably be dead. For a long time I thought that was what I deserved. Like I'd dodged fate or something because I'd gone to get Don's food. Part of me always thought it would catch up to me eventually, but so far I've survived.

We end the call and I walk back into the cabin.

Aspen is awake and sitting up in the bed, leaning against the headboard. Her citrus scent dominates the room and both soothes and arouses me. The light from the morning sun bursts over her, gilding her dark brown hair and making her eyes sparkle when she looks over at me.

"Who was that?"

"Aro. We're going to them."

"Oh. Okay." She breaks eye contact with me and looks down at her hands. "I was kind of hoping this part never had to end and it would all go away on it's own."

I move onto the bed and take her hands, massaging her fingers as we talk.

"I wish. Maybe when it's done we disappear again."

Aspen looks up, confused. "You'd do that?"

I can't look at her because everything I'm feeling would be too obvious, but I keep working on her fingers as I speak. "I know that you don't want to settle in Chicago, and honestly, I don't want the city. I know that if you're willing to be part of their family, it'll be on the periphery. I'm okay with that. I don't have anything to go back to." I swallow heavily and look up at her. "I want to go where you go."

Pink creeps up Aspen's cheeks and she looks away from me to try and hide her smile.

"Yeah, that sounds good." Her voice is a little raspy and I hide my own grin.

"Let's get packing." I lean forward and plant a kiss on her forehead before I leave the room again and start getting all our things together. It's only been two weeks but we acquired a lot of random crap and I put it all together as fast as I can. Now that there's a destination in mind, the itch inside me to get going and face the fight is a constant irritation.

Roger Forrester messed with the wrong family. Depending on how this goes, the remaining Forresters might find themselves wiped off the map.

I pack everything in Aspen's Land Rover, and she gives me a wave before heading off into the woods to exercise Troy for a bit before we're stuck in a vehicle for a few hours. My phone buzzes with a text and it's coordinates from Harp. Luckily, it's only about a 4 hour drive until we can meet up with him at a roadside diner.

We wander through the little cabin we called home for a bit one more time, making sure we didn't leave anything behind. I feel like I'm leaving with something essential to my existence. Aspen ducks into the bathroom, but looks over her shoulder at me with a slight, crooked smile.

God. Damn.

I have to fists my hands at my sides to stop from grabbing her. From putting her up on the kitchen counter and fucking here there one more time. I swear she can read the fantasy in my eyes.

I lock up the place and put the key in the lock box. Aspen curls up in the back with Troy's head on her lap, stretched out and trying to relax. I think having confronted her past with her sisters over the phone has been easy; she's about to have one of those conversations face to face and I can tell she's anxious about it. I let her be in her own head for now, and focus on the road.

Once we get back onto a major highway, I have to be more vigilant.

A little over halfway through the drive, a gray SUV starts working its way through the traffic and getting closer to us. My back straightens, my senses go on alert, and I watch as it matches my movements. The driver is trained, but is likely assuming that I wouldn't notice someone following us. The highway isn't packed but it isn't empty either, and most of us are heading the same directions.

"Aspen," I say her name a few times before she wakes up. It's important that I stay calm. She adjusts so she's sitting up, and her sharp eyes immediately catch the change in my demeanor. "We're being followed."

"What do we do?"

"I need to get away from other people. I'm going to take the next exit." I meet her eyes in the rear view mirror. "I need you to do whatever I tell you. Please." Not that I don't love her fierce and independent spirit, but I need to trust that she'll do what I ask so I can operate the way that I need to.

"Okay."

"Promise me. I need to know that I don't have to watch for you."

"I promise," Aspen nods. I hold her gaze and I have no choice but to believe her.

I take the next exit where there's nothing listed - no gas stations or food. Just an exit to back roads and farm land. The SUV exits after me, and it doesn't take long for them to drive closer.

The SUV speeds up and I don't, wanting to maintain control of my vehicle to engage in evasive maneuvers. There's a bend coming up in the road and I'm hoping that I can pick up speed after it, and that if I brake just right they'll go off into the ditch at the side.

"Hold on."

I start to go around the curve as they catch up to us and tap my bumper. In return, I tap the brakes. The Land Rover lurches and there's a crunch as we're hit in the back.

But my plan works.

The SUV has to slam on their brakes and they start to lose control, sliding into the ditch on the side of the road.

Unfortunately, they clip the back end of the Land Rover and we slide, spinning around in the middle of the road until we're facing the wrong way.

I put the rover in park and get out, unholstering my weapon and sliding off the safety.

"Stay here," I command, and open the door.

I use it as a shield, gun aimed, watching the SUV for signs of life. There's no movement for a long moment, and then a man gets out of the front passenger seat.

The second I see the weapon in his hand I shoot. He goes down in a spray of blood and I wince hoping that Aspen isn't watching. That she doesn't see me like this while I do the work necessary to keep us safe. I will kill without hesitation because that's how I was trained, but it's so much easier to do it when I know I'm doing it for her.

The rest of the car doors open and men spill out, armed and trying to stay low as they come up the side of the ditch. Luckily, I am very good at what I do and I don't have room to show them mercy. I know who sent them, I know that they're either here to kill or take Aspen, and I won't allow either to happen.

I turn off my mind and drop back into training and muscle memory. I shoot. They fall. Four total.

Still in my switched-off mode, I approach the vehicle. The doors are open and I can easily see inside - it's empty. They're all dead. Threat neutralized.

I search the SUV, grabbing cell phones and documents, as well as searching each body for the same. I don't look at the injuries I inflicted. That will come back to me later, when I feel guilt for taking a life in hindsight. Even when I know it's the right thing, I don't relish it.

I don't regret a second of my training when I look in their trunk and see rope and duct tape. They would've taken her, and they weren't too worried about the condition she was in. Rage boils through me and I want to turn to the nearest body and empty the rest of my clip into it, but our resources are finite at the moment. I need to handle business and get back to Aspen. Get her somewhere safe.

When I'm done searching, I go to the back of the Land Rover. There's some dents and scratching but it's a tough car and still drivable. I open the back hatch with a little bit of work, and put everything I grabbed into one of the bags for us to look at later.

I still can't look at Aspen. There wasn't a hint of fear in me when I was facing down men with guns. Now, there's a nearly visceral terror that she might look at me differently after seeing what I'm capable of doing.

Instead of going to her, I turn away and send a text to Harp. We're going to find somewhere to lay low and delay our meeting. I've got to get rid of these bodies, or at least delay anyone finding them. He texts back immediately, and tells me not to worry about it, just send my coordinates and get the hell away as fast as possible.

I take a deep breath and return to the driver's seat. I turn to look at Aspen. Her eyes are wide and Troy is sitting in her lap, covering her with his furry body. She glances to the side, and then meets my eyes.

"You good?"

"Yeah," she answers, terrifyingly soft. "Are you?"

"Yeah." No. Not even a little.

"What now?"

At least she trusts me enough to ask me that. Before I can answer, my phone buzzes again. Harp sent me a location of a motel not too far from where we are, and said there's already a room waiting under the name of one of my fake IDs. I start the Land Rover and start heading in the right direction. It runs with no issue at all.

"We lay low. Meet Harp tomorrow."

"Okay."

It takes all of my control to keep my eyes on the road instead of looking at Aspen to analyze her reaction. She's silent, barely even breathing, and staring down at Troy as she pets him. He's calmed down now that we're moving again.

I glance in the mirror and Aspen's eyes meet mine, her brow furrowed. I would give anything to be able to read her mind right now. There's no disgust or derision in her expression, and no fear, which is a relief, but she's thinking about something. Aspen is processing the reality of what she knew with what she saw, and I can only hope that math works out in my favor.

When I pull into the motel and park, she stays in the Land Rover while I go in to the office and get the key to our room. Aspen still says nothing when we go inside. She leaves Troy to snuggle up on the bed and goes into the bathroom. There's tension in every line of her body, and a blank mask for an expression.

I sit down on the lone chair in the room and put my head in my hands. All I can do now is wait, and hope that she'll talk it through with me.

26

Aspen

I stare at myself in the small mirror above the small sink in the small bathroom. The motel room isn't bad, but I need a moment without Gailen or Troy to be alone with my thoughts and feelings. I don't want to be soothed or numbed, I need to feel this.

When Gailen told us to stay in the rover, something dropped over his expression that was both familiar and foreign, and in the moment it scared the fuck out of me.

I saw justified violence in his expression.

I knew he was going to leave the car and kill those men. I watched as he killed them with almost passive precision. There was nothing but control in every move he made. He was efficient, a max of two shots for each of the men in the SUV.

The way he moved was so restrained, so strong. He walked up to the SUV and searched them like he felt nothing. Gailen was a force, and I could not keep my eyes off him.

When he came back to the Land Rover, my heart was racing, my body reacting to both the fear of the men coming after us and to what I had watched him do.

It wasn't like I was unaware that Gailen was capable of violence, especially when he was coming from a place of protection, but it was different to see it. It was different to see who he became when he thought he was protecting me.

How I felt about it changed when I saw, clearly, when he met my eyes that the only thing on his mind was making sure that I was okay. That he hadn't scared me. Despite the toll I knew it would take on him and how much he'd blame himself for us ending up in that position, the only thing he cared about was that I wasn't afraid.

While I had seen the mask of violence take over the faces of other people, it had never been in a situation where that violence had been used to protect me. Elton often wore the mask of justified violence but it was chaotic, unrestrained, and without control. Seeing it like this, and used only as a last resort, was on another level. This was a first.

I try not to lie to myself, and a small gasp comes out of my mouth as I allow myself to feel the truth without shame.

Gailen doing what he did was hot. Like panties soaked, heat across my skin, heavy breathing because I'm so turned on hot.

I'm more worried about my reaction to his violence than the fact that he is capable of it. If I'd had more awareness of what it was that I felt, I probably would've pushed him down and fucked him right there in the middle of the road, dead bodies be damned. He'd killed for me.

I thought it was hot that he saved me, but killing for me? Sexy in the extreme.

My heart is still pumping hard and insistent, the beat of it in my throat, my chest, and my clit. I am so aware of every inch of my skin and I want to leave this tiny bathroom and rub myself all over him. I want him to fuck me, own me, and command me, knowing that he is capable of extreme violence and also knowing without a doubt that he would never turn that violence on me.

That might be the thing that makes Gailen so appealing to me on every level. I know what he could do to hurt me, but I know that he never would. Not on purpose. That level of trust and safety is priceless to me.

I leave the bathroom and his head lifts up from where he was holding it. There's a moment where he looks devastated, and my heart squeezes. Gailen thinks I'm upset. I don't blame him for thinking that I was pulling away. I did, for a moment, to retreat inside myself and figure out what I was feeling.

He keeps his eyes locked on my face, even as I push my shorts and panties off to pool at my feet. I walk over to him and lean forward, forcing him to lean back on the chair. I undo his belt, then his pants, and yank them down his body, lifting his hips before he can protest.

Gailen's cock springs free, hardening as I look at it. I meet his eyes and reach for him, stroking his warm length and feeling him thicken at my touch.

"What are you doing?" he groans out, thrusting into my hand.

"Thanking you properly," I whisper back, not sure why I'm being so quiet. Watching his hesitation, understanding the power I have over him right now, is incredibly arousing. My pussy had clenched and dampened at the first shot he fired, and I'd only been getting more worked up with every minute that passed. I was drenched for him.

I suck his half hard cock into my mouth and take him deep, gagging as he gets harder with each stroke of my lips and tongue. He tastes so good and I want to thank him like this every single day.

Once he's fully hard, I move to straddle him in the chair. There is just enough room for me to rest my legs on either side of him.

Gailen gasps when I press his head to my entrance and he learns exactly how turned on I am by all of this. He slides inside me easily, spreading me open around his thick, hard cock and I whimper the deeper he goes. My eyes squeeze shut as I impale myself on him until my ass is resting on his thighs.

I open my eyes and meet his gaze. He's trying so hard to maintain control and not touch me; he's letting me do whatever I want to him.

"You kept us safe," I say quietly, and start to slide my hips back and forth. I cup his face in my hands and stroke his cheeks, then slide them up into his soft, silky hair. Loving him with my touch. It all feels incredible. Gailen's hands fly to my ass and he grips me, but doesn't try and control my movements.

"I've never seen you like that," I moan and then lean over so I can talk directly into his ear. "I liked it."

Gailen pulls back and meets my eyes, searching for the truth, and I start moving faster, feeling my orgasm start to build as I work myself on his cock.

"Did you like seeing that I would kill for you?" he finally grumbles, gripping me hard and moving me on him, deepening each stroke.

"Yes," I whimper, and my hips get jerky as I squeeze him with my inner muscles.

"I would do anything for you," he rasps, getting into the moment with me. "There's no limit."

"None," I agree.

"I would never hurt you," he says as he leans in and sucks on my neck. I cry out again, almost to the edge. "But I would hurt anyone for you."

It's sick, but it gets me there. My entire body tenses as I start to come, riding him as bliss spreads through my body. Gailen wraps his hand around my throat and pulls me to him, his tongue diving into my mouth and tasting my moans. He pushes me away and my back arches, changing the angle of him inside me.

Gailen holds me there, hand around my throat, not cutting off my air but controlling my movement, and thrusts his hips up. He looks down to watch where we're joined, and I watch him watch us. Lust and darkness cloud his expression, and I am struck once again that I have this powerful and deadly man beneath me, subservient to me, and desiring me so much that he would do anything to keep me safe.

No one has ever cared enough about me to want to protect me like that.

No one has ever wanted me, without question or condition, the way that he does.

I throw my head back as he presses up into my body, hitting deep inside me and sending pleasure radiating from my core. I gasp when his hand pulses around my throat, but then he lets me go.

"On the bed. All fours." His voice is a rasping grumble that I feel inside me, but I do as he says. I slide off of him with a little moan and move to the bed. I take off my shirt before I climb on, resting on my forearms as I pull up my knees. I'm raised up and spread open for him.

Gailen teases me, sliding the head of his cock along my slit and making me whimper in demand. I scream when he slams inside me, filling me up in a way that steals my breath. Every thought leaves my head, and all I can do is feel.

I relish his hands on my hips, fingers digging into my soft flesh. The feeling of my ass jiggling with each thrust, the tension in my thighs and calves as the pleasure slides through me, the scrape of the comforter against my cheek. Even the way my throat feels raw from the sounds escaping me. I want it all.

"Anything for you," he grunts out before pressing deep into me as he comes. I moan and flutter around him, the pleasure of knowing I'm filled with him gives me an extra shiver.

Gailen collapses next to me and I fall to my side. I squirm as I feel the mix of our come on my thighs.

"You sure you're good?" he asks, moving my hair out of my face and caressing my cheek gently. His softness and concern make my heart twist even further. I cannot imagine existing without him anymore. I want to be his soft place, that he can fall into after doing what needs to be done.

I don't regret running because I got to be this person, in this place, and experienced and survived things that made me into the woman I am. I can't regret a single thing because I wouldn't be here otherwise. Even the hurt and the torture of my early life, because I don't think I could fully appreciate Gailen without it.

"I'm perfect," I answer him, and snuggle closer to press a soft kiss to his mouth.

27

Gailen

Aspen and I cram ourselves into the small shower in the motel room to clean up. It mostly ends up with her groping and grabbing me, and I get to hear more of her rusty, high laugh. I love the smell of her soap on my skin, and being able to breathe her in whenever I want.

I'm surprised that I sleep at all when we climb into the bed, but I wake up the next morning feeling refreshed. We don't have far to go, and Harp sent a text that as far as he can tell everything is all clear.

We take Troy for a quick wander around the yard of the motel to do his business, and then pack ourselves back into the Land Rover.

"I've loved this thing, but I think it's time to get rid of it," Aspen sighs. "Start fresh, down to the car."

"You don't want to go back to your place in Wyoming?" She loved it there. I could tell that even if she was isolated, she was at peace. Obviously, I'll have to give it some security upgrades.

"Will that be possible?"

I contemplate her question, and play out this situation to it's logical conclusions.

"If Roger is dead, then there's no one to come for you. The men after you are motivated by money not loyalty. Without him, no one will be after you. You could go back." She nods at my response and then falls back into a contemplative quiet. Troy sticks his nose over the console and bumps her. She pats him absentmindedly and he retreats, assured that she's fine.

"I want to go back."

Then I'll find a way to make that happen.

Harp is waiting for us in the parking lot of the diner, leaning against the back of his Jeep with his arms crossed and his frown mask on. Harp has a resting frown, a frown he uses to keep people away from him, and an actual frown from being mad. This is the keep people away frown. Not that there's many people around this diner, or any of them that seem stupid enough to approach him.

I give him a nod, and he returns it, before locking his intense gaze on Aspen.

"Hey," she says with a tremor in her voice.

He nods at her, then drops his gaze to Troy.

I'm stunned when Harp squats down and claps his hands, inviting Troy to him. Aspen pats Troy's head and the dog trots forward. He smells Harp first, then drops his head for pets. Harp looks the most relaxed I've ever seen him when he's not with Aro. He digs into Troy's fur and scratches him behind the ears. Troy's tail waggles with joy.

Harp looks up and meets my eye, then tilts his head, letting me know to move our stuff into the Jeep. He stands up and lets Troy go, then opens the back. I do the same with the Land Rover and move everything over.

Aspen stands with her hand on Troy's head, stiff and uncomfortable. She's nervous, I can see it in the way the lines are forming between her eyebrows as she tries to close in on herself. Harp literally isn't going to say anything, but somehow that silence might be more difficult for her. It's not like he can easily let her in on his thoughts.

She committed to making the phone calls and clearing the air, but that's very different than seeing any of them in person. Not only is she going to be in a small, enclosed setting with Harp, when we arrive she's going to see Aro for the first time in four years.

Harp holds open the door and gestures for Troy and Aspen to get in the back. The dog goes first, and Aspen waits for Harp to step away. They have an awkward standoff and he tries to give her a smile but it's more like a grimace. It's impressive he makes the effort, but I'm not sure Aspen knows that. When he steps away to round the car to the driver's door, her shoulders fall in relief.

Before she can get in, I step close to her, still out of Harp's view.

"It's okay. I'm with you."

Aspen rests her forehead against my cheek for a second and inhales deeply, then lets me go and gets into the backseat. I move into the front passenger seat and finally fully relax because Harp is one of the only people I feel physically safe around. I'm tough and I'm lethal, but I've got nothing on him. I trained to be this way by choice, he was molded by life to be this person.

While we drive, I update him on what's been going on since I first got back to Aspen's cabin. I leave out our deeper personal connection, but Harp has a thing for details, as does Aro, so I don't think our tie to one another is going to remain a secret. Harp listens as I talk, and when I glance behind me, Aspen is leaning back against the seat with her eyes closed. She's feigning sleep but I know she's not, she's listening to my interpretation of everything that's gone on.

Like my belief that the vet we paid off didn't keep the information about her to himself, and probably doubled up on his reward. He'll pay for that in other ways another time. The men I saw at the diner who made me uneasy, and that they were the same men who approached the cabin when we escaped. Only two of them were in the SUV that tried to run us off the road, which means they're part of a larger team.

The few weeks of running, hiding, and researching. We're well-rested and ready to fight, and even though I know overprotective is the Sorrelle standard operating mode, neither Aspen or I will let that happen. This is our fight in general, but it's Aspen's fight more than anyone else's. It was her life, her uncle, and her revenge that got her in this situation. She has earned the right to clean up her own mess. It's not even connected to the Sorrelles except through her; Roger hasn't made any moves against them. He only wants Aspen. That's the leverage I'm going to use to get him in my cross-hairs. When I'm done, Harp nods. That's all I'm going to get. When I look back, Aspen is genuinely asleep now. Troy has his head in her lap and is taking a nap himself. They are safe. We're going to fight. It's all that's keeping me going.

When the Jeep turns into the driveway that's nearly hidden by trees, I feel even more secure. I don't know that I would've seen the turn off until I'd driven past it.

Eventually, we emerge from the treeline to a huge open field, and on the far side is a big glass and wood house. Aro and Henry are already standing on the deck, waiting for our arrival. Harp probably has this place alarmed and sensored within an inch of it's life to keep those two safe.

Henry is bouncing up and down, his dark hair is a spiky halo around his rather giant head. I know he's a toddler but that thing is enormous.

Harp can't keep the smile off his face as we get closer, the corners of his mouth turning up just a bit. Troy stands up in the back, his tail wagging, as he sees new people. I turn back to give Aspen a reassuring look and to remind her again that I'm here. She's not alone. I'm not going anywhere.

She gives me a grudging smile but her eyes are tight and dilated.

When the car stops and we emerge, Troy dances in place, waiting for Aspen's permission to explore the surroundings.

"Is he safe to run around?" Aspen asks. The first thing she's said to Harp since we parked at the diner. Harp nods, and she pats Troy. He immediately goes running around, then back to her, then around again.

Aro picks up Henry and carries him down the steps toward us. She's tiny, and he's almost half her size already.

"Hi," she smiles, looking between Aspen and I. "Welcome. Come on in."

Henry smiles too and nods. Then he arches away from Aro and makes grabby hands for Harp. Harp takes him and walks toward the house and inside without a look back.

"Do you need help with your stuff?" Aro offers, shoving her hands in her hoodie pocket.

"Nope," Aspen says and pops the p, then whirls away to open the back of the Jeep and start piling our bags into her arms. I share a look with Aro and then shrug. It'll get better with time, I have to believe that.

I join Aspen in grabbing our bags, and we follow Aro into the house. Troy trots after us. She directs us to set down the food we brought in the kitchen for her to take care of, and then leads us straight upstairs toward the bedrooms.

"That first door is the bathroom, then the next two are the guest bedrooms. Harp and I and Henry are at the end of the hallway." Aro waves toward the last doors on the left and the right. "You can pick who gets what room."

Aspen blanches. "We only need one room." I hear Aspen's breath whoosh out of her as she realizes what that reveals about us.

Aro was mid-word and stops, her mouth frozen in an O. She spins and turns to look at me. "Really." Her expression is so neutral I have no idea how to interpret it. I sigh and shut my eyes for a second to clear my thoughts. I didn't think about the sleeping arrangements, so

Aspen and I didn't talk about it. We should have.

Aro stares between us, but Aspen is in front of me so I can't see her reaction.

"Okay then. I'd recommend this room, it has the king bed." Aro indicates the room on the right, after the bathroom. Aspen nods and steps into the room. I move to follow her but Aro stops me with a single finger pointing at my chest. "We will be talking about this later."

"Yeah, I figured."

She frowns at me but then leaves us to our own devices.

We don't say anything as we settle our things down, and Aspen sits on the end of the bed.

"Sorry," she cringes.

"It's okay. I didn't think to talk about it. Do you want them to know about us?"

Aspen gives me a real smile for the first time. "There's an us?"

"I would fucking hope so." I sit down next to her and pull her into me, then fall back on the bed. She shifts so her head is nestled in my shoulder and she can look up at me while we talk.

"What does that mean?" Aspen's voice is small and uncertain. "I've never been part of an us." It's almost sweet.

"Anything I've ever been involved in before doesn't compare to you," I tell her honestly. "I meant it when I said I belong to you. I'll go where you go. There's no one for me but you, and I will do anything for you. Anything you ask, it's yours. All I ask in return is your honesty."

"What kind of honesty?" Aspen moves so she's straddling me on the bed, and I'm surprised by her shift in mood. I thought she'd be more apprehensive being here. "Like the way I enjoy licking your sweat from your neck?" She leans over me and tongues my pulse. I'm getting harder by the second.

"The way that even when you make me come so many times I can't move, it's not enough?" Aspen ghosts her lips across mine and I feel them move as she speaks. "I will never have enough of you."

I thrust my hand into her hair and yank her down to me, parting her lips and savaging her mouth. Aspen moans softly and grinds on me, her core so hot I can feel her through our pants.

"Take me," she whimpers. "Quick, quiet," she begs and then shimmies away from me.

I sit up and watch as she slides her shorts off and half way down her thighs, and I start undoing my own pants when she bends over the bed. I slide my fingers through her, and she's fucking soaked. As I line my cock up with her entrance and start to push in, I reach with my other hand to cover her mouth.

"Take it quick and dirty," I growl, and then push all the way into her. Aspen moans against my hand and her back arches, giving me room to press deeper. Keeping a hold on her face to cover her cries, I start fucking her at a fast and brutal pace. The sound of her arousal as I move through her is carnal and delicious. The scent of her pussy invades my senses, and I swear if I could find a way to eat her and fuck her at the same time, I would.

I reach around to put pressure on her clit, and Aspen tightens around me, her whole body stiffening before she crashes over the peak into an orgasm. It rips my own out of me with a muffled groan. I hold her to me, her back to my chest, hand still over her mouth, as I fill her with my come.

"I've got you," I promise her as I let her mouth go. Aspen pants but rests against me, as if she can't get close enough.

"Yeah, you do," she laughs.

28

Aspen

Aro and Harp keep looking at us, and then exchanging infuriating looks with each other. Gailen warned me, in case I'd forgotten, that they basically communicate by telepathy. Aro is attuned to microexpressions naturally and Harp is detail oriented because of his job as an assassin, but I still have no idea what they see when they look at us.

Since it's out in the open, Gailen doesn't hold back or hide anything and I appreciate it more than I expected. He touches me casually, sits close to me, is always considerate of me and checking in on me. I've never had someone take care of me in that way. There's never been an opportunity for it.

After we eat a delicious lasagna for dinner, Aro pulls out the board games. We eventually agree on Trivial Pursuit because between the four adults in the room we have a wild and broad array of knowledge.

It surprises but pleases me when Henry toddles over and climbs into my lap. I haven't been around kids much but I like them. Kids are way easier than adults. I adjust him slightly and he leans back against my chest. Aro opens her mouth to say something, probably to tell me that I can give Henry to her or Harp, but Harp stops her with a hand on her thigh.

I let Henry roll the dice for my turns and whisper my answers to him before saying them for everyone to hear. He's warm in my lap and I feel like I understand him in a way I fear understanding the adults in my life. Henry is simple. He wants to feel safe and comfortable, and he doesn't understand the dynamics of the situation. I don't even know if he knows I'm technically his aunt.

It doesn't matter to Henry. His instincts tell him I'm safe person, and that's a huge compliment in my book.

We play through and Henry burrows into my lap and puts his head down on my thigh.

I don't realize that I'm stroking his soft head until I catch Gailen watching me. Watching us. There's an expression on his face that's heated, but not in a sexual way. In my mind, I see a flash of a future dream, where the baby sleeping in my lap is ours. I wonder if that's what he's thinking too.

Aro clears her throat and our gaze breaks.

"Let's take a break so I can put him to bed." She nods down at a heavily sleeping Henry. Aro moves over to me and slides her hands under his warm body. Henry whimpers a little but relaxes as soon as his head is on his mommy's shoulder. I watch them walk away, envy heavy in my heart.

Despite how I grew up, I would be a parent if the opportunity arose. I know so much about what not to do that I think I could raise someone healthy and strong. Someone who would believe that they could rely on their parents, be safe, until they were ready to find their place in the world.

You're good with him, Harp's electronic voice comes from his phone.

I smile tentatively. "I like kids. They like me."

He gives me his version of a smile in return.

When Aro comes back into the room, Harp turns toward her as if she spoke, his gaze drawn to her presence. The love and contentment between them is palpable. Harp isn't hiding his scar, which is still mangled and red, and Aro's expressions are so big and clear they dominate the attention on her face. It takes a second to even register the fading pink slash across her cheek.

Harp looks away from her to look at Gailen, and jerks his head toward the door.

"We're going to go talk in the office," Gailen says. "You good?"

"Yeah," I nod and swallow around a lump in my throat. Gailen presses his forehead to mine and then kisses it, reassuring me with his touch. I close my eyes and breathe in, taking in the mix of his scent and my grapefruit body wash. I love the way we're mingling together like that.

I don't watch them leave, but focus on cleaning up the bits and pieces of the game and putting them where they belong in the box. I'm not sure if I'm preparing for a lecture or an interrogation when it comes to Aro, but I brace myself for either. I school my face, trying not to give anything away.

Aro sits down on the couch and waits patiently. I can feel her looking at me, but I don't look at her.

Finally, there's nothing left to delay me, and I move to sit down.

Aro and I stare at each other, both in poses of relaxation on opposite ends of the sofa.

She breaks first and starts laughing. "You're not in trouble, you know."

"I'm not?"

"Definitely not with me, but honestly, not with any of us." It's weird to me that she speaks on behalf of her family, but I know how close they are so maybe it's not. I'm sure that I've been a topic of frequent discussion over the years.

I shake my head, struggling to believe it. These people risked their lives for me, and I turned my back on them. Aro has always felt like the most approachable of them without the emotional baggage I have with Anora, so I decide to be open with her.

"Why not?"

To my surprise, she laughs. "God, you're so much like Aster sometimes. Nature doesn't have shit on nurture." Aro covers her face with her hands for a second, calming herself. "You spent your life thinking dad rejected you, and you'd been a captive since birth. Even if it hurt to lose you when we'd only just gotten you, I don't think any of us weren't sympathetic to why you ran. We sorted through our feelings about it because at the end of the day, we wanted you to feel like it was safe to come back when you were ready."

"That's insane. That's too healthy."

Aro laughs again. "Probably. Anora made us do a lot of therapy."

I flinch at her name and of course Aro doesn't miss it. "What was that?" she asks.

"I hurt her the most."

"Maybe," Aro shrugs, "but I think it was more disappointment than anything."

"Gee, that makes it so much better," I deadpan.

"She wanted to give you the life you missed out on, and it took her a bit to understand why that wasn't what you wanted. You two have the most in common, in a way. Both of you were hurt by that asshole. You bonded in a moment of trauma, and believe me when I say that she forgave you first, once she understood that your way of dealing didn't have to line up with her way of dealing and that was okay."

That soothes something inside me that I didn't know was twisted up. I nod, accepting what Aro is telling me, even if it will take me awhile to truly absorb and process it.

"So, you and Gailen, huh?"

I look away from her, trying to hide my blush. It's not like I grew up telling anyone about my crushes and I've never had a relationship.

Even when I was taken off guard by my attraction to Tuck and we hooked up, I never told Si, my closest friend in the collective. Luckily, Tuck never told anyone either or I would have had to kill him. There has rarely been a time in my life where I could talk about my feelings outside of therapy, but in the last few weeks it seems to be all I'm doing.

Talking to Gailen about every thought and fear that crosses my mind, every emotion that impacts my heart. Now I'm contemplating talking to Aro about my romantic feelings for the man that hunted me down.

"Yes," I settle on replying primly. Aro grins at me.

"How'd that happen?"

I stare at her, searching her gaze for judgment. "I don't know. The second we were in the same room together, physically present, I felt… something." I run my hands through my hair. "I'd seen him hundreds of times in surveillance and didn't feel that way, other than you know, being a living breathing human who can see he's hot." Aro nods in agreement. "Then boom, face to face, and it's like my entire being realigned to his."

When I snap out of it and look at Aro, her gaze is soft. "Yeah, I know what that's like. You're sure it's not - a savior complex, or the adrenaline of the situation?"

I snort in derision. "The thing happened before the adrenaline. We were fighting our feelings before some dudes attacked my house." I think about what she said about a savior complex, and how we might be drawn to each other because of that strange, dark moment in our past that haunts us both. We're physically scarred from it. It's not surprising there are mental and emotional scars too.

"I can understand the savior complex idea, but if anything, I was mad at him for saving me. I was angry at him for a long time, Aro, and my own therapy got me to let that go. Our past would have had me pushing him away, not letting him in."

She stares at me for a long time, eyes picking through my expressions and reading me, the small perma-smile she has resting on her lips. "Okay. Do you want to talk about that?"

"No," I admit. I do not want to talk to Aro about how I thought I deserved to burn to death with my brother. How sometimes I think a piece of me is still suffocating inside that cabin, endlessly inhaling smoke and waiting to immolate. That on the dark days, I still wish Gailen had left me there. Living and healing hurt more often than not, and if I was dead I wouldn't have to deal with any of it.

If I was dead, no one would be in danger right now.

But I'm not, so all I can do is move forward and make the best choices that I can.

"Did you date before Harp?"

"Definitely not," Aro answers. "Why?"

"How did you know how you felt about him? That it was real and not just," I pause and search for something that doesn't sound insulting. "Puppy love?"

Aro looks down at her hands and silence stretches between us. It's not uncomfortable because she's genuinely trying to figure out how to answer me. That's nice. It's nice that she's taking that question so seriously. I know that I'm younger than all of them, and that they probably still see me as a kid even though I'm not. Not even a little bit, and maybe I never have been. Still, I'm usually confident in my feelings.

I'm not confident about falling in love.

"It was less about the butterflies, and more about trust." Aro shifts on the sofa and her gaze gets dreamy as she reminisces. "Harp's hot as hell so of course I wanted to jump him, and I enjoyed the way being attracted to him made me feel, but it was the other things that made me fall, and told me it was real. We understood each other, I could tell him anything and know that I'd be met with openness and sincerity. I could have good days and bad days, and so could he, and it was never work to take care of each other. It was something we wanted to do because that's how much we mattered to each other.

"I've been sober for almost five years, and there's been temptation, but I love myself too much to screw up. I got that from Harp. You should never be sober for someone else - you have to want it for you, and I think love is like that, too. You know it's real when the person you love gives you reasons to love yourself."

The smile pulls at the corners of my lips before I can catch it because what Aro said makes sense, and it makes me think of things Gailen has done and said that made me feel exactly that way. His acceptance of my revenge on Roger, on what I do for a living, the way he is proud of me for finding a way to survive, for the way I ran and hid and taunted him for years, rather than being angry about it. Gailen makes me love myself for exactly who I am, and that's powerful.

I wonder if I make him feel the same.

It's not in my nature to be expressive, but I think I do need to show and tell him how amazing I think he is, and that I would never have played the game I did with anyone else. They wouldn't have been worthy.

"Well, that settles it for me," Aro sighs and leans forward to slap my knee. "I approve. Team Gaspen."

"That's a terrible portmanteau."

"Too late, it's out there, it can't be stopped. I still call Issac and Aster Freelaster, although that one is her own fault. She made the joke, I have no reason to let it go."

I laugh with Aro and yet another weight lifts off my shoulders. It's going to be okay.

That's the moment I realize that I had this entire conversation without relying on Troy for comfort. I know he was in the house, but I look around and don't see his brown fluff anywhere.

"Have you seen my dog?" I ask Aro.

She looks back at me and nods. "He's, uh, sleeping on the floor next to Henry's crib." Aro pulls up a camera on her phone and shows me an overhead view of Henry's room. Sure enough, Troy is curled up on the floor. A pang of jealousy shoots through my heart, but it's also really sweet.

"I can go get him, if you want?" Aro offers, but I shake my head.

"Nope, I'm good. He'll sniff me out if he needs me." I stand up and stretch. "I'm going up to bed. Thank you, for - well, everything."

Aro nods and watches me as I leave the living room and go up the stairs. My limbs feel heavy as I get ready for bed. Even though that conversation went well, it still took a lot out of me.

I'm mostly asleep when Gailen comes to bed. He pulls me into his warm body and I drift back into a deep, dreamless rest. Maybe I'll never feel a hundred percent safe, but this feeling is pretty damn close.

29

Gailen

We recover with Aro and Harp for three days. It's like a vacation.

Aro has been trying to get me alone to talk about Aspen, but I've been avoiding her. I don't want to talk about my feelings with anyone else. I know that she and Aspen talked about us because Aro and Harp stopped exchanging looks whenever Aspen and I interacted, but that was a conversation between sisters.

Aro is my friend, and she means a lot to me, but my feelings for Aspen are complicated and entwined with our current situation even when I wish they weren't. They are tangled with pieces of our shared past that we've talked about, but the air still hasn't been cleared. Aro isn't the person I want to talk to about this. When the time comes, talking about my feelings is only for Aspen.

Harp seems to intuit that, and knows his wife well enough to know she's too much of a romantic to keep her nose out of a story like ours. He's been running interference.

I get it though, why Aro thinks we're romantic. It is kind of a fairy tale - a huntsman falling for his prey and vice versa. Not to mention having permanently scarred my body to save her as a kid. The history of us literally written in our flesh. It's dramatic and sweeping and even

I could get caught up in the romance. Maybe after we're all safe.

It's been a gift to be here, though.

Aspen, Henry, and Troy became a little gang of woman, boy, and dog. They go everywhere together. Henry still wants his parents to put him to bed and if he needs comfort, but if he is awake, he wants to be with Aspen. It's precious and bewildering, but she seems to be taking to it like she expected it. They seem to have their own language and way of communicating in little sounds and fits and starts.

They play together, build blocks, knock things down, and read books, all under the watchful, adoring gaze of a fluffy mutt.

Fuck, it makes me want to fill her up with my babies, and we can raise our children together in the middle of nowhere just like this.

I never thought kids were going to happen for me. I was never even sure I wanted them. Now, the idea of a Aspen carrying our baby, years from now, fills me with both arousal and a heart-racing amount of joy. It makes me feel nostalgic for something that hasn't even happened yet.

My imagination races me through being by her side for every milestone, of delivery, of holding a tiny new life made of both of us, of us being odd but awesome parents, playing games, cuddling, laughing at the mess, celebrating holidays, loving each other and passing that love on to little people who have pieces of our hearts.

I want to see her reflected in our children. I want to see her heal another piece of herself by giving her own kids the freedom and choices that she never had, and always being a safe place for them to land.

Aspen seems comfortable with Aro, too, and I think that when things come to a head, and they will soon, she'll be going in with an ally.

In my estimation, Aster is on her side, Alina is cautious, and Anora is the unknown.

Anora is always the unknown. The most secretive, the most defensive, and the one with the most terrifying husband. He probably has the smallest body count of the men in the room but Owen is both an unstoppable force and an immovable object. If he thinks anything would harm Anora, his reactions aren't rational.

I get it now.

I think I'd do some pretty irrational things to keep Aspen safe and happy.

Aro's phone rings while we're eating dinner, and when I see Owen's name on the screen, I know it means that our rest is done.

"You're on speaker," Aro answers.

"Roger is in Chicago. He landed a few hours ago."

"What's the move?" I ask. Aspen is stiff beside me, instinctively leaning toward me and putting her hand on my thigh. I put my hand over hers and weave our fingers, binding us together.

"Start planning to get here. I'll let you know if he reaches out."

"You think he will?" Aro asks.

"If he thinks we have Aspen, yes." The tone of his voice tells me that there's something he's keeping to himself, and I don't like it. Owen ends the call without another word.

Roger Forrester is making more moves to get Aspen. Given the way he was treated the last time he interacted with the Sorrelles, he must really be desperate for revenge if he's willing to be in their territory. He wants Aspen, and he's determined to get her.

It terrifies me.

It activates the violence inside me, and I know without a doubt that I would tear that man apart with my bare hands if it meant keeping Aspen safe. If it means setting her free from the bullshit of the Forresters.

We all share a look, and even Henry notices the tense silence between the adults.

"Excuse me," Aspen says, her voice unsteady, and she leaves the table and runs up the stairs. Without saying anything, I follow her.

She's pacing in the bedroom, one hand pressed to her face while the other opens and closes like she's squeezing something invisible. I watch her for a second, absorbing what she looks like when she's overwhelmed. It will help me catch signs of it in the future.

I step into the room and close the door. Aspen turns to me, and there's a mix of agony and fury in her eyes that I understand completely.

"This is my fault."

"No," I answer immediately. "All of this started before you were even born."

"I could have let it go."

"Then you wouldn't be who you are. You didn't want a bad man to have more power to hurt people. Whatever happens, what you did was worth it."

Aspen's arms drop to her sides and her shoulders droop. "You really believe that, don't you?"

"Yes. Unequivocally." I take a step closer to her. "Your family feels the same."

She winces.

"They see you as family. Give it a try."

I reach my hand out to her and she steps closer, reaching back. I pull her into my arms and hold her, feeling content when she buries her face in my neck and wraps her arms around my waist.

"Do you believe me?" I murmur into her hair.

"Which part?"

"Either. Any."

"I know they see me as family. This is still my fault. It's my mess to clean up."

"That might be true, but that doesn't mean you have to clean it up alone. No matter what, you've got me."

"Yeah, I do." She tilts her head up and kisses my pulse. It races beneath her touch. Things have changed so quickly and yet I can't regret a second. I went from hunting her with annoyance and frustration in my mind to being overwhelmed with a need to be near her. I've never been in love before but I think this has got to be pretty close. Even if it's only been weeks, my instincts know. They call to her, they always have, I just didn't understand what they were saying until now.

"Let's go kick his ass," she laughs and pulls back from me. Aspen lifts a little to kiss me, and I kiss her back, inhaling her presence.

Mine.

30

Aspen

While we've been packing our things, Harp and Aro have been preparing to go as well. Because I rushed off, we never really talked about what was going to happen next, or how Gailen and I were going to get to Chicago.

When I come downstairs, Aro and Harp are standing close in the kitchen, and she's talking quick and quiet. Harp is nodding, but I can see the tension in all the lines of his body. He cups her face, and then presses his forehead to hers. I don't need Aro's ability to read people to understand the emotions passing between them.

I clear my throat as I step off the stairs so they know I'm there. I've already heard Aro during the nights we've been here; I don't need to see her getting railed in the kitchen, thank you.

Aro turns with a smile, but I can see her anxiety. "I'm going with you. Harp is going to stay here with Henry."

"You don't have to come, stay here with your family."

Harp and Aro both give me a look that's so similar I start laughing. The same frown, the same head tilt, the same furrowed brows.

"You're my family, too. I'm doing this."

I nod because I know there's no use in fighting them. "Thank you."

"We all want to kick some Forrester ass. You're just the excuse." Aro steps around Harp and starts putting things into a large purse. She's whispering to him quietly, probably hashing out details together.

I walk into the living room where Henry is sitting on the floor playing with his blocks. Troy is behind him, letting Henry lean on his warm, soft body. My dog has a new buddy, and given everything that's going to happen, I think we have to part ways for awhile.

Tears well in my eyes as I kneel down by his head, and press a kiss to his soft muzzle. Troy's tail thumps against the floor but he doesn't move to stand up, protecting the baby next to him over coming to me. It hurts but I do love it at the same time. If I have to leave Troy, I want him to be somewhere safe, and where he'll be loved. He's got the freedom here like he did at home, and I'd hate to try and shuffle him through Chicago.

I'd hate for him to watch me walk out the door, and never come back.

At least here, he's got Henry.

As if passing the torch, I fluff Henry's hair and he gives me a wet, toothy smile.

When I look up, Harp is standing a few feet away, watching us.

I walk over to him. "I'm leaving Troy here."

Harp nods.

"If I don't..." I trail off.

Harp nods again, and I appreciate that he's not going to try and make me be optimistic about how this might go down. There's every chance the rest of them will be fine. The one that Roger wants to punish is me. If he tries to make them choose between me or themselves, I'll sacrifice myself before I let any kind of fight happen. That's the way it has to be.

I turn my back on the silent giant and sit back down on the floor with Henry to enjoy the last beautiful moments with...my nephew.

I let myself think it. Let myself think of him as part of me, belonging to me, my family. He's easy to love because there's no baggage. Just us, hanging out on the floor, smashing towers.

I have to admit that Aro grew on me fast. That I do think about what it would've been like to be her little sister growing up, and how different of a person I would be. I love her, and even Harp, in a strange friendly kind of way. I don't love her like a sister, but I could see myself getting there someday.

If I make it through this, I promise to let myself try.

Doesn't mean I'll succeed, but I vow to be open to the possibility. To maybe trust them the way they deserve, and not hold myself back from them so fully. Before Gailen, I don't know that I would have been able to believe myself capable of that kind of change. Trusting him has opened me up to another side of myself.

Gailen and I wait outside as Aro says goodbye to her family. His warm arm is wrapped around me and he's tracing shapes on my back with his fingers, soothing me without being obvious about it.

"What if something happens to them. Any of them." It's not a question. It's a fear given power because I'm voicing it out loud. "I'll never be able to forgive myself."

"Stop blaming yourself for other people's choices. They know the chances, the consequences, and this is the choice they are making. Trust me, you can deny them until you're blue in the face and it won't make a difference. You could run, and they'd do it without you."

Gailen turns me toward him and waits until I meet his eyes. "Do you want to run?"

I shake my head. "No. I want to end this so I never have to run again."

His gaze softens and everything inside me goes warm at the expression, like I said exactly what he wanted to hear right then.

"No more running." He takes my mouth and I open for him, letting all the tension drain out of me as his tongue teases across mine and sends a shiver down my spine. My hands dig into his t-shirt and I press closer, deepening the kiss.

"Oi!" Aro shouts. "Get a room."

Gailen and I laugh into each other's mouths and I love the intimate familiarity of that. We break the kiss and get in Aro's car. She opens the driver's door but before she gets inside she stops and looks at the house. Harp and Henry stand on the deck and wave. She blows them both a kiss before climbing in, and as we drive away I can hear her sniffle from the backseat.

"I'm fine," she reassures us. Gailen turns to look at me, and reaches back for my hand. I take it and he squeezes mine twice, quietly reminding me that it's her choice. I can't control other people's choices, I can only shape mine around keeping them safe.

I let his hand go and burrow down into my hoodie to pretend to take a nap, and avoid the emotions that are starting to overwhelm me from every direction. By tomorrow we'll be in Illinois, and I'll be entering the Sorrelle compound for the first time in my life.

The fear rockets through my stomach, and I push it aside.

That's a reality to dwell on later.

31

Gailen

The tension in the car increases as we get closer to the Sorrelle compound. Aspen sits up straighter and straighter, her jaw is clenched so tight I can see hollows beneath her cheekbones, and her knuckles are white where her hands are gripping each other. Aro keeps looking at her in the rear view mirror and her frown gets deeper with every glance.

Anything I want to say to Aspen I don't feel like I can in front of Aro. Not because she'll be offended but because honestly, it's between me and my woman. It's for her to hear, and it's private. Aspen would want it to be private.

As we pull up to the gate, I put a hand on Aro's arm.

"We need a minute."

"You got it." Aro gets out of the car and I follow suit, moving around to the driver's side. I wait to see what Aspen will do as I watch Aro approach the guard at the gate. She greets him and he lets her in. After an audible breath, Aspen exits the car and re-enters in the passenger seat. I drive away, heading toward nothing but putting space between us and the compound.

"This is a lot harder without Troy."

"I'm not as soft, but you can pet my hair if you want."

I'm surprised when she takes me up on the offer, reaching over and sliding her hand into the hair at my nape. The tips of her fingers tease my scalp and she pulls just enough to make my cock take notice. Wrong timing, but if it's making her feel better I'll make sure she doesn't see how her touch is impacting me.

"Talk to me, baby."

Aspen nods but doesn't say anything. She watches the road ahead of us, teasing her fingers through my hair as she collects her thoughts. As we drive, I remember there's a park not far from where we are, and I start heading in that direction. It will be a quiet place for us to stop and talk, and we won't have to do anything or head back there until she tells me she's ready. Whether it's an hour or tomorrow morning.

We have to face going there eventually, but I'm not going to rush her. I know she's afraid of seeing Anora, and I'm not going to invalidate that.

The park entrance comes up and I turn in, but Aspen doesn't notice. I wind along the park road until I see a small parking lot, mostly shielded by trees. Despite it being a nice day, there are no other cars parked in it.

Before turning off the car, I open the windows a little to let in some fresh air. The scent of wet trees and pavement sneaks in, and I take a deep breath. I've always liked that smell. When I look over at Aspen, her eyes are closed and she's doing the same thing. Her hand drops from my head and she relaxes back into the seat, some of the tension leaving her body.

"I don't know how to explain why I'm afraid."

I don't say anything because even though I wouldn't be able to help her find the words, I understand her fear all the same.

"I was beaten over the head with the idea that they're the enemy, and even though I never believed that, it still infected me. I disconnected from my thoughts and feelings when I did things for him that I knew would hurt them. It made me feel like a monster."

She runs her fingers through her own hair and groans.

"My therapist reassured me that it was necessary for my survival, and I *know* that's right, but it doesn't mean I *feel* it." Aspen sighs. "The other problem is that they want me to be part of their family, and that might be too much to ask of me. Being friendly? Clearing the air? Sure. But I am not a Sorrelle sister."

I nod and turn away from her to make sure she can't read any reaction on my face.

"If things had been different, if Don had known about me..."

Guilt gnaws at me. I wonder if he hadn't been killed how things would have been different for Aspen. Would Elton still have taken Anora? Probably. The thing is, even if Don had been alive and opened his arms to Aspen and accepted her, proved her brother's lies wrong, I still think she would've run. It wasn't about the Sorrelles, it was about the Forresters. It was about recovering without any pressure or input from anyone about who she wanted to be and how she wanted to live her life.

Aspen accomplished that. Now it was a choice to belong to a family.

The Sorrelles didn't see it as a choice though. To them, she belonged, simple as that. I was envious of that, but my experiences with them were different. My beliefs about family were different than hers.

"I still would've run," she finally says.

"I know." I reach over and take her hand, and she lets out a small laugh of surprise.

"I don't like the idea that I owe anyone without it being a conscious choice. Blood is only so thick...and while I like all of them, I respect them, maybe even love them a little, and I think with enough time I could trust them, there's always going to be distance. I might be present but never fully a member. Does that make sense?"

"Yes," and I mean it. "It's not like you can replicate childhood bonds with them, and even if they know what you went through, knowing and *knowing* are not the same."

"Exactly. Will they hear me? Really hear me?"

"Aspen, you're never going to let anyone step on your boundaries ever again. The thing I want to know is why are you doubting yourself?"

"I don't want to hurt them." Her voice cracks and she presses a hand over her mouth, squeezing her eyes shut to fight the tears. I reach across the console and pull her to me, inhaling her, forcing her to mimic my deep breaths, calming her with my touch.

"I don't think you will. I don't think they'd put you in that position. All they want is an open line of communication, not a promise signed in blood."

Aspen gives a watery laugh and pulls back from me to look me in the eye. "Make me stay and talk. Don't let me run."

"If you run, I run with you. That's the best I can promise."

"I'll take it."

We come together, foreheads touching. I trace my fingers up and down her thigh, letting her take all the time she needs. It's a perfect bubble of a moment, and if we're being honest, then I need to be honest, too.

"I'm in love with you."

Aspen's eyes snap open and she pulls back to search mine. "Why?"

To be honest, that response doesn't surprise me. I doubt she's ever thought about anyone loving her, let alone being in love with her. Despite Aspen's healthy ego in terms of her abilities and accomplishments, she doesn't think that loving her is possible, even easy.

"It's not something I chose," I laugh. "But even if it was, I'd still choose you. I am in awe of you. Challenged by you. Satisfied by you. The world seems less dark when I'm with you and I hadn't even realized I was missing the light."

Aspen closes her eyes and leans on me, taking in what I said. I look out the window and watch the sunset, bursts of red and orange across the sky. It's like her. Brightness that fades into the dark. She gives so much light to my life it hurts to look at, but I would follow her into the darkness with no hesitation.

"You're insane," she murmurs.

"Probably."

"I'm in love with you, too." It's the gentlest thing I've ever heard her say. Like she thinks if the words come out of her mouth they're going to break.

I smile before I can stop myself and when she looks up at me, she pokes my cheek in a teasing way.

"Glad we got that out of the way," she sighs. "Let's get this over with so I can jump on your dick sooner rather than later to celebrate being idiots in love."

"Anything for you." I give her a hard kiss before turning the car back on.

32

Aspen

Fuck, fuck, fuck. Even though I feel like I have a better handle on things, and there's a tiny delighted fire inside me because Gailen loves me, the nerves about going to the Sorrelle compound dominate everything else. It's not just the people, it's the entire place.

Gailen is steady beside me, his presence reassuring. While I know a ton of data on everyone inside that house, he actually knows *them*. His lack of worry or concern, his persistent belief that they will understand rather than suffocate me, does help with my anxiety. If Gailen kept working for them after everything, it was more than because he believed he owed them. It means he believed they were worth owing in the first place. Gailen is loyal, but not indiscriminate with that loyalty.

They are good people. It's clear on paper that they are. They don't just talk - all of them act on what they think is right.

Do I deserve to be around good people? I wouldn't describe myself as a good person. The things I do are mostly motivated by a selfish desire for isolation, even if I do hurt bad people. Even when I take down those who hurt others, I do it the way that I do because I don't want to have to interact with the rest of the world.

I don't want this large network of humans that will want something from me, even if it's because they care about me and it's coming from a good place. They know I'm broken. They saw it. They felt it. My brokenness has already hurt them in the past. All any of this is doing is opening them up for more emotional hurt from me, and a chance at real physical harm if they take up my cause against Roger.

I'm not worth it, not for them.

I don't mean that I'm worthless as a person, because I know I'm not. Am I worth it to Gailen, and is he worth it to me? Hell yeah. But the greater Sorrelle family? Hell no. They don't know me or owe me and I wish they'd stop thinking that way. The pressure is too damn much.

That's why I'm really here. It's to get the information that they have, and to make sure they understand that I will handle it. I don't need them to clean up my mess.

I don't need them, period.

I want to set them free, the same way they freed me.

Maybe in a world after dealing with Roger, I can learn to want them and accept them on equal terms. In that world I can learn to have carefully boundaried relationships with them. But I refuse to let another asshole Forrester man force me to bond with any of them.

I couldn't help myself with Aro.

I also won't deny the draw and connection I've felt with each of them.

It's just an inopportune moment to establish an adult relationship with my estranged sisters.

We pull up to the gate and the guy inside nods at Gailen before pressing the button to open it up. He tilts his head and gazes at me curiously, but I don't meet his eyes for longer than a second. It's taking all I have to hold it together right now.

I'm relieved when no one is waiting outside when we park in the curved driveway. It gives me another moment to prepare myself.

"You got this?" Gailen asks. I swallow thickly and nod.

We get out of the car, and he rests his hand on my lower back as we walk to the door.

"Do we knock?" I whisper, but before Gailen can answer the door swings open.

Anora smiles at me, looking like she was barely held back from running out the door when we pulled up. She steps out and yanks me to her, hugging me against her small, slim body. I don't hug her back. Mostly because where she's hugging me has my arms trapped against my sides, but I also don't know if I would have even if I could move. I feel weird.

Glancing over her shoulder, Owen is standing at the threshold and I can hear other voices behind him.

It does seem very clear that Anora isn't mad at me, and that is a relief to know. It does not, however, make me feel any less awkward. I'm not a hugger, so I kind of hope the rest of them don't expect it of me.

Eventually, Owen clears his throat and Anora lets me go. She can't take her eyes off me as we step into the house. For some reason, I can't bring myself to look around. I don't want to familiarize myself with the what ifs it inspires - what if Don had known about me, what if I'd had a chance to grow up here, what if coming here today was returning home rather than a first arrival?

Too many what ifs that drive like a knife into dreams I've buried alive.

A dream where I belonged with a family that loved me.

I still want a family that loves me but I'm not sure I can build that with *this* family. There's too much ugly history and pain between us all. We'll always be tied to each other, and I've been in denial that I can ignore that tie, but it's not the same as being each other's true family.

I want a true family with Gailen.

Even if we start the whole thing as a family of two.

That's a wild feeling for me. The man told me he's in love with me and now I'm all, okay let's be a family and make babies. But I also won't deny the idea of having our own babies fills my chest with a pleasurable press of emotions. Like a new dream is being born inside my heart. Our babies. Our life.

The me I was 6 weeks ago would be shocked.

I follow Anora and Owen into the living room, my senses seeking the feeling of Gailen close behind me as we approach. The voices die down as everyone turns to look at us, the only remaining chatter is the noise of the kids playing in a group by the fireplace.

"Uh, hi?" I greet everyone. Attempting to take some kind of control.

Aro gives a wave from her spot on the floor with the kids, and Aster and Isaac give me matching nods from where she sits on his lap on a chair.

For the first time, I see Alina and Derick in person. She stands up from the couch and Derick follows suit. They walk over, and the power in her body is still obvious even though she no longer works security or even practices much martial arts anymore. She's like a panther that was forced into human form. Derick looks more subdued, and I understand. He's been betrayed by family before, it doesn't bother me that he's reserving judgment about me.

"Hi. How was the drive?"

"Not bad," I answer. "How was the flight? I didn't think you'd be here."

"I'm not missing a chance to fuck with Roger Forrester," Derick says quietly, glancing to make sure the kids aren't paying attention.

"Dinner is soon," Anora interrupts, "relax for a few minutes while I get things ready."

I give her a nod and head toward Aro and the kids. Without introductions, I know who they are. Bran, the baby, is on her lap, and his sister Siobhan is playing some sort of game with the twins, Malcolm and Adelaide. The oldest two, Wyn and Rianna, are paging through a giant book on dinosaurs and slightly hiding behind the couch.

I move toward Siobhan and ask what she's doing.

"Matching."

We play together, and the twins hand us random cards to add to our pile as Siobhan looks through the stack for the matching picture. Gailen stayed by the door, and when I look over to check on him, I realize he feels as uncomfortable as I do even if it's for different reasons.

He's an employee, and this is a family matter. He's welcome, but not truly part of it all.

Siobhan breaks my eye contact with him by crawling into my lap. She grabs my face and turns it toward her.

"Read." She hands me one card at a time and I read the word on it that tells her what each picture is. Siobhan tells me if she does or doesn't like something with each card, and I get caught up listening to her high sweet voice and giggling with her about what she likes.

Anora comes back in to the living room. "Why don't we get your things settled before dinner and it's too dark out."

I slide Siobhan off my lap, and stand.

Gailen and I walk out and grab our things out of the trunk. We stuffed most of our clothes in the same bag and our toiletries in the other. It hurts for a second that I'm not unpacking anything for Troy. I miss my dog even though I know he's safer where he is right now.

Anora and Owen lead us upstairs, and my feelings of awkward anxiety return. It's one thing to be in the places where visitors are welcome, it's a different thing to be in their private spaces like the bedrooms. It's like I'm seeing the house naked or something.

"We're putting you in Owen's old room," Anora says over her shoulder. "It's been empty for years and we don't actually have guests that often."

Owen opens the door to the room and we all step inside. The room is dark but still cozy, and Gailen and I put our bags on the ottoman at the end of the bed.

"Apparently, this is the room where they store the surly orphans," Owen jokes dryly. Anora looks scandalized, but I laugh, because he's not wrong that I am both surly and an orphan.

"Gailen, your quarters downstairs are open," Anora says, and it hits me then that Aro didn't tell them anything. I'm both pleased that she'd keep it a secret, but also stressed that it would have made this all so much easier if she'd blabbed.

"No, he's staying with me," I blurt, not thinking about the bomb I am potentially dropping. I just know that I can't stay here without him close to me. There's no possibility of me putting up a front until we can talk about it. The panic that squeezed my heart at even the idea that he wouldn't stay with me was horrible.

Anora freezes mid-word, and her eyes narrow as she focuses on Gailen.

"What?" Her voice is thin and false, because she heard it, she just doesn't like it.

"Gailen stays with me," I answer more firmly.

"Seriously?" Anora practically snarls. Owen reaches for her but she brushes off his arm as she charges up to Gailen and makes an attempt at getting in his face. It would be comical if I wasn't feeling defensive already. "We trusted you, and you prey on her when she's vulnerable?"

"It wasn't like that," he replies, but I hold up my hand to stop him.

"I'm an adult," I remind her. This is another fight that's mine.

"You're 19," Anora says in a pleading voice, the anger dropping off her face as she turns to me.

I turn to Gailen because I don't know how to deal with this without saying horrible things, and that's not how I want any of this to go. My hand automatically seeks out his.

33

Gailen

Anora can't keep her gaze on Aspen, even though Aspen is trying to handle this for herself. Anora's feelings about this situation, and blame even though there isn't any to place, are focused on me.

"Get out of my house." Her voice is firm, but she's not the person I take orders from. Not anymore.

Aspen steps back and grabs my arm, and I can feel her vibrating with tension. Her anxiety is skyrocketing and she's scared. This isn't anger, her jaw would be clenched, this is borderline panic. Anora doesn't even realize the line she's walking right now. She has no idea the damage she might be about to do.

I take Aspen's hand, and that seems to piss Anora off more.

I shoot a look to Owen because he might understand how precarious this is. Just because Aspen has been going along with everything so far, she is one wrong move away from disappearing again and Anora is blinded by her own feelings right now. Aspen is not the same broken kid we rescued four years ago.

"Anora," Owen starts, but she whirls on him. They share a look I don't understand.

"We should go," Aspen says quietly, and flinches when Anora turns back to her, her back bumping into my chest. It makes my own fury rise, and I want to pick Aspen up and carry her out of here. Instinctively, I shift so that she's standing slightly behind me. Anora doesn't miss the move.

"You're worried that *I* would hurt her? You're the monster who took advantage of her when she was alone and inexperienced. Did you always want this? Did you agree to track her down just to get close to her? Did it take four fucking years because you were trying to keep her away from us?" Anora's voice has gotten louder and higher with each word. "Is this you punishing our family?" Her voice bellows and I can hear footsteps in the hallway.

"Punishing you for what?" I ask, something cracking inside my chest that I didn't know could still break. "For forgiving me? Taking care of me? Trusting me, giving me purpose? What the hell is wrong with you?" My voice cracks and shame fills me because I've worked hard to never show the Sorrelles how vulnerable and indebted to them I truly am. It made me weak if they knew that I needed them. Aspen clings to my arm, her nails digging into the skin grounding me to reality.

I hate that this is how it's playing out. That she's going to choose me over them, without even giving them a real shot.

"That's enough," Owen starts but gets interrupted when the whole crew, minus Aro, busts open the door and piles into the bedroom

"I should go," I turn to Aspen, and decide to ignore whatever the fuck is going on with Anora. I'm not going to take this chance with her family away from Aspen, and right now decreasing the tension is all that matters. I cup her face, pretending as if there's no one in the room but me and her. I make her look at me, make her come out of the place she's retreating to and demand for her to see and hear me.

"I'll be back. You're safe here." I press a kiss to her forehead and inhale her sharp grapefruit scent. Quiet enough that only she can hear, I add, "I love you."

169

Then I walk out the door without looking at any of the rest of them, and I don't stop until I'm back in Aro's car. Every step away from her physically hurts me. I'm meant to be by her side, but I'm trying to do right by her, too.

Sitting inside the car, it hits me hard and my rage burns from inside my skin and I scream. The sound is muffled by the car but I know that I won't be safe to drive until I get it out. My hands are wrapped around the wheel and it's creaking from how hard I'm squeezing it. When it's all out, my throat is raw and raspy. It aches from the power of my own voice.

I don't know where to go.

There was the search, the finding, and then I would go wherever Aspen went. I have friends here in town but we don't speak often, and it's not the kind of friendships where I can show up in distress. Everyone else is business contacts and allies.

That's when I know I've got one place to go.

I drive into the city.

I don't know what's happening and part of me is afraid that I'm driving into my own disappearance. They have so much more for her than I could ever offer, and Aspen belongs with them. She is one of them, even if she tries to deny it. They look alike, act alike, even think alike. Her and Aro were immediately drawn to each other the second they spent any time together.

A nearly tangible connection exists between the sisters when they're all in the same place. Aspen won't be able to fight the truth of that forever.

The neon lights of the club are almost comforting as I approach the door. I haven't been here in nearly a year, but the bouncer is the same guy as always, and lets me in with barely a glance.

It's packed inside, as usual, and I make my way through the crowd to the VIP area. There's a guy there I've never seen before with a clipboard.

"Gailen Burke." He looks down at the list, at me, and then moves aside so I can enter. There are far fewer people here, and I take a seat at the bar. The bartender looks at me for a long second and then pours me two fingers of whiskey, neat. Smart assessment. I give her a nod and take a sip.

Someone sits down next to me, and based on the size of the shadow I'm going to assume it's Patrick, not Dinah. They probably clocked my arrival the second I stepped inside and were waiting to see what I would do, and what I was here for.

The redheaded enforcer doesn't look at me when I glance over, but does signal the bartender for a whiskey.

"Haven't seen you in awhile," he lilts.

"Haven't been around."

"Still hunting women?" There's a taunt in his voice, but we've always had this relationship. Patrick and I met before he officially worked for Dinah, and before I worked for the Sorrelles. He's a year older, but at the time we met we were both lost, and the mercenaries that pulled us in trained us well. I've seen blood with this man, and we can't even acknowledge it out loud.

When anyone pressed if or how we knew each other, we would always attribute it to running in the same circles.

Not the truth, which is that I knocked out one of his canines when we were sparring once and I'm the reason he had the chance to replace it with a silver tooth. Or that he field dressed a stab wound to my leg when we were trying to rescue a kidnapped kid. That we watched a close friend get his head blown off, and had to leave his body behind if we wanted to survive.

"Found the woman. Kind of want to keep her."

"Ain't that some shit?" He takes a large swig of his whiskey and gives me his approximation of a smile, the silver canine just visible beneath his top lip. "Then why are you here?"

"Not everyone wants to let me."

"Ah. Always knew those fuckers were snobs." While Patrick tolerates Aster, he never warmed up to the rest of the family.

"They aren't," I get defensive immediately. "I don't blame them for how they feel, but it's kind of shit how they reacted."

"It is. You need somewhere to crash?"

I finish my whiskey. "I don't know yet."

"There's space upstairs. Dinah's out, so I'm in charge."

"Out?"

"She had a fucking baby."

I turn to him, mouth agape. Dinah had finally married Seamus Brennan a couple of years ago, but both of them had always been pretty openly anti-kid. Especially when Seamus came from a blended family of eleven children.

"The kid is cute as shit, too."

"I wish I'd recorded that. Mean you want to settle down and have one too?"

Patrick looks off into the middle distance, his eyes unfocused, and I'm stunned. Not only is he genuinely contemplating it, but that kind of look tells me that he's already got someone in mind. Of everyone I've ever known in my life, he's the last person I would have expected to end up in a committed relationship. Never was a man more of an island than him.

"Maybe."

"Fuck."

"Yeah."

My phone buzzes and I see a text from Aspen.

A: *Where are you?*

A: *Come back.*

G: *Things settled?*

A: *All clear.*

I tip my empty glass against Patrick's.

"I'm safe for now."

"Offer stands if you need it. Good luck."

Hopefully, I won't need it.

34

Aspen

It takes me too long to crawl out of the fear and panic that keep me frozen and chase after Gailen. Anora gets in my way and blocks me from leaving the room.

"Let him go."

"Get out of my way." I keep my voice calm because this is not the time to snap at anyone. I take a few steps back and away from all of them. This is what I was afraid of - that it would be all of them against me, and I don't have Gailen here to back me up. Even if he'd make the situation worse by standing with me.

"Aspen," Anora starts, her hands up like she's trying to calm me. "You are caught up in all of this, and Gailen crossed a line. This is where you need to be."

"Don't tell me what I need," I barely restrain my hiss.

"You're so young, Aspen, you don't know-" Anora keeps saying my name and it's pissing me off, but her trying to tell me who I am is so much worse.

"I'm not young, I've never been young. You are the one who doesn't know, Anora," I spit her name like a curse word even though it hurts me. All of this hurts me, more than they can imagine. "You have no idea what I've been through and who it's made me, and you have no idea what I want or what I need."

"And whose fault is that?" She snaps back. Alina and Owen both step up to hold onto her, trying to calm her down.

"Mine!" I shout back at her and open up my arms, ready for their anger. "I made a choice and I accept the consequences because I did what I needed to survive. But I'm tired of just surviving. Gailen makes me want to live."

"Gailen is almost a decade older than you!"

"Oh my god, Anora, you're my sister, not my keeper! Fuck off!"

Anora's mouth snaps shut and everyone is staring at me, a weird tension in the room. I take that as my opportunity to make a break for it and storm toward the bedroom door. It slams behind me as I race down the stairs.

Gailen is probably gone, and I don't want to wander around outside, so I turn away from the living room before Aro can see me. I can hear her talking to the kids, and I can't handle her sweetness right now.

Instead, I find myself roaming down hallways and turning in random directions until I follow a light in the back corner of the house. I step into a long, skinny glass room. It's a mix of a sun room and a conservatory, since it's filled with plants. There's a cozy bench immediately to the left. If someone glanced in, they wouldn't see me unless they stepped all the way into the room. A perfect hiding place.

I curl into a ball on the bench and lean my head against the exposed brick wall. My heart is racing but I also feel really proud of myself. It was a difficult conversation, an argument that broke down into yelling, but I also hope I got the point across. I am not a child, and no one is going to make decisions about my life for me.

My life is mine. I belong to me.

I don't know how long I sit here with my eyes closed, but I feel something shift in the air and snap my eyes open to see Isaac stepping inside. He closes the door to the room and moves over to sit with me.

"Not who I was expecting, if I'm being honest," I tease.

Isaac smirks. "Honestly, I'm just the one who found you first."

I nod in response.

"All of us, the ones they chose, were hurt by our family in one way or another. If anyone understands your hesitation, it's us."

"I know. I know all about all of you."

"Oh yeah?" He laughs. "What's my last name?"

I tell him and he pales a little. When I tell him his brother's name and the country he's currently covertly stationed in, he holds up a hand to stop me, and starts laughing.

"Fucking hell, you're dangerous." He shifts on the bench to look at me. "Their bond and the way they feel about family can be intimidating, I get it, and I don't agree with Anora here, but I also think you don't believe that they care about you. That they want you in the family."

"They want me in the family on their terms. That whole thing just proved they won't hear me when I say what I need if it's not in line with what they want."

Isaac nods, not disagreeing outright. "Maybe. Give Anora a little time to adjust and to stop feeling like every time she blinks she's going to open her eyes and you're gone."

"Fair," I frown but agree.

"You know why they freaked out before you ran off, right?"

If he's talking about the weird tension before I left the bedroom, then no. I shake my head.

"You called Anora your sister."

My stomach turns over. "Oh."

"What you said, that whole argument really, that's how sisters argue. That's how they argue. You acknowledged what you are to each other. It wouldn't surprise me if she's bawling her eyes out with joy right now." He laughs slightly and shakes his head. "The fact that it's Gailen you've gotten all wrapped up in doesn't help."

"Why?"

Isaac looks at me and narrows his eyes, assessing. "Did you know he had a thing for Aster?"

I laugh. "Yeah." We talked about it for all of five seconds and then he got so embarrassed about it that I left it alone, out of respect.

"The thing I've learned about the Sorrelles is that they have some kind of magic, and I think you got it too. When it comes to love, fate is on their side. Like Gailen knew he was meant for a Sorrelle and misplaced his feelings until he found you. I didn't believe in fate until Aster but I know that my entire life led me to her. I'm with her until it kills me, and I couldn't be any fucking happier. I belong with this family."

"And Gailen doesn't?"

"No, he does, but he doesn't see it. He's been part of the family for a long time but refuses to accept it. You two have that in common - convincing yourselves that you don't deserve this family when you might more than anyone else."

"Fuck off," I huff and look away, my chest aching at the thought.

"It's all coming full circle. All that fate shit again. You're bringing each other in."

"We'll see, I guess."

"I guess. Come on." Isaac stands up and moves to the door. "Everyone is in the living room. Let's clear the air."

I take a deep breath and follow him out of the sun room. He leads me down a hallway and we only make two turns before we're back in the front of the house. Apparently, I wasn't as lost as I thought. Everyone is in the living room, and as soon as I step inside Aro stands up and rushes over to me.

"You good?"

"I'm good." I turn and address the room. "I'm good, but I will not be having any conversation with anyone that tries to talk me out of my relationship with Gailen."

"I'm just worried," Anora says quietly, and I can't look at her. I'm still hurt.

"You didn't see them together," Aro comes to my defense. "I already interrogated it, trust me." She laughs and gives me a one-armed squeeze. Not quite a hug, but an act of solidarity that I don't mind. "You need to chill."

"I'm in favor," Aster speaks up, focused on Anora.

"Alina?" Anora looks over at her sister.

"You are not seriously voting on my relationship right now." My anger is rising again.

"No, we're voting on whether or not Anora needs to shut up about it," Aro assures me.

Alina looks at me. "Do you know what he did after high school?" I nod. "Then I'm good. No one could keep her safer."

"Ugh. Fine," Anora throws up her hands. "I'll keep my concerns to myself."

"You guys are weird." I cross my arms to protect myself, my skin crawling with discomfort. "I love him. I need you to get that. He's not going anywhere, but if he goes, I go too."

Anora's gaze softens when I meet her eyes. "I'll get over it, it's a lot at once. I'm sorry. I shouldn't...that wasn't necessary."

"I know. But I'm not the only one who needs to hear it."

"Right," she nods and slaps her thighs. "Get him back here. We're all good."

"Can we eat now?" Wyn pops his head into the room, snapping us all out of it. There's a ripple of laughter and everyone gets up to go into the dining room. I hang back a second and text Gailen to come back to the compound.

The first conflict has been handled, apparently. I can't say I understand the way they work and think, but I feel weirdly supported at the same time. I'll feel even better when Gailen is back by my side.

35

Gailen

It's dark when I get back and let myself into the house.

Aspen is sitting in the living room watching the fire, and turns to me with a smile when I step into the room. She shifts on the couch and pats the spot next to her. When I sit, she lifts up my arm and pulls it around her, snuggling into me. We don't say anything for awhile, letting our bodies settle and relax now that we're together.

I didn't even realize how tense I was from being away from her.

There was a buzz beneath my skin that stretched out to a gentle hum now, the feeling of her dancing through my veins. Aspen is like a physical extension of myself, and I can't exist the same way if I'm far from her. Our breath syncs and I feel her inhale to speak before she even says a word.

"We sorted it out. There was some yelling but I think we all got there in the end. Even had a nice family dinner." Her voice gets a little snarky there, but I know it's a defense mechanism. "I told Anora to apologize to you."

"She doesn't have to, I understand." I kiss the top of Aspen's head.

"I know. I do, too. That doesn't mean you aren't still owed an apology."

"Whatever you want," I murmur.

"Gailen…" Aspen trails off and I shift so I can see her face and try and figure out what she's thinking. Something else is very clearly on her mind, and it must be big if it's overruling her processing the conflict she had with her family earlier today.

"You're wrong about something," she finally says.

"Me? Never."

Aspen softly headbutts my chin. "You said I belong only to myself, and while it was true at the time, it isn't anymore. That's what I realized tonight. I belong to you. All of me. Good, bad, twisted, free…it's yours. You are the only person I've ever met worth giving all of myself to, and you have it. I'm not saying it as an offer, it's a fact."

Something inside of me is pressing to get out, and I'm worried right now that I'm going to cry in front of her. I don't know the last time I cried, but being given something so precious, so hard-won, from her is almost more than I can take. I try to inhale but my breath gets caught in my chest.

Aspen sits up, concerned, and immediately crawls into my lap. She straddles me and presses my head to her chest and squeezes me tight. I'm not crying, exactly, but I'm breaking in some way. I inhale her sharp citrus scent, inhale the subtle undertone of her skin. Her heart beats against my cheek and I can feel her chest expanding and contracting with each breath.

She is alive and perfect, and she is mine in a way I never expected.

A way that I never planned on, but wouldn't give up for anything in the world.

This right here is a world of two, and it's only the beginning.

"I love you," I murmur against her before pressing a soft kiss to her collarbone, and then up to her neck.

Aspen makes a satisfied hum. "I love you, too. I think I've always loved you."

She pulls back and looks down at me. "Did you know Issac thinks all the Sorrelles are blessed by fate to find their soulmate?"

"And he thinks I'm yours?" We'd all teased Isaac for his belief that he's fated to be with Aster. The other guards found it a perfect thing to give a rather terrifying person shit about, but he'd always smile and let it roll of his back because at the end of the day, Aster was unequivocally his. They owned each other. I'd never seen her bend for anyone but him.

"He does."

"What do you think?" I press a quick kiss to her lips.

"I think it's time for you to take me upstairs and show me what belonging to you means." Aspen bites my lip and then shimmies off me, dancing away with a suppressed giggle. I follow her up the stairs, both of us groping each other in the semi-darkness as we move down the hallway to the bedroom. When I get inside, I close the door and lean against it, staring her down.

"Take off your clothes," I tell her, voice a low whisper.

Aspen peels off her shirt, then drags her hands up her stomach until she cups her tight breasts. I'm already hard, but my cock throbs when I watch her pinch and play with her own nipples through the thin cotton.

"Off," I command again. She obeys. "Lick your fingers, and keep playing." She obeys again, wetting her fingertips and hissing as the moisture makes the air cool on her nipples. "Pinch and pull, baby, hard, until I tell you to stop." Aspen methodically works her breasts, doing as I said and squirming as it turns her on. Her eyes never leave me, but she's dazed and horny.

I step toward her and undo her shorts, then slide the denim and her panties down her legs. On my knees before her, I look up and watch her play as her nipples turn into hard, dark peaks.

"Don't stop," I remind her, before parting her pussy lips with my fingers and revealing her clit to me. I lean close and blow on it, causing her to flinch, but she doesn't move away from me. She smells fucking delicious, and my mouth waters as I tease us both with my proximity to her cunt.

Something has been unleashed inside me when said she belongs to me. A dangerous, possessive darkness that wants to own every single inch of her. That wants to pull her into a depraved place alongside me where pleasure is our reason for everything.

I point my tongue and press the tip into her clit. Soft at first, circling it gently, over and over until I can see her thighs shaking as she tries to stay still. I tease her as I run my hand up the inside of her leg, until I'm pressing my fingers into her entrance.

Aspen's knees give out for a second and she groans when she impales herself on my hand and it presses her further into my face. When her hands drop to my head I pull back.

"You stopped." I shake my head and pull out of her. Aspen whimpers but she's trying to hide the smile on her face. "Were you a bad girl?" I ask.

Aspen nods, her cheeks turning pink.

I stand up and walk over to the bed to sit down. I pat my lap.

"Lay down and take your punishment."

She walks over and stretches her tight body over my thighs, centering her stomach over my erection and bent just right so her little bubble butt is right where I want it. My left arm rests across Aspen's shoulder blades, holding her down and still, as I use my right hand to smack her ass.

The gasp that leaves her is satisfying, and I wait to see if she'll tell me to stop.

She doesn't.

I spank her until her ass cheeks turn red and I can feel her grinding and dripping onto my thigh. She's so wet it's soaked through my jeans.

"You took your punishment like such a good girl," I tell her as I run a hand down her back and then over her abused skin. It's such a lovely shade of pink, almost as sexy as the color of her cheeks when she blushes. "Now you get a reward."

My fingers slide easily inside her, and I press them against her g-spot, working it hard and steady as she writhes on my lap. Seeking release, her hips buck fiercely.

I'm shocked when she bites the comforter to muffle her cries as she comes, more of her dripping onto my clothes. I slide my fingers out and lick them clean, the sweet with a hint of tart driving me crazy.

Aspen lays limp on top of me, but I'm not done with her. I roll her over and cradle her in my arms, standing up to turn us around and place her on the bed. I take off my clothes and climb over her as she reaches for me, languidly pulling my mouth down to hers.

"Fuck me, Gailen. Own me," she whispers against my mouth before sliding her tongue inside to tangle with mine. I shift my hips so I'm aimed at her core, and slide inside her indescribable, perfect heat. Aspen moans into my mouth and I swallow it down as I start to rock my hips against hers.

I'm going to make her go over the edge at least one more time before pumping her full of come. Then I'll let her rest, and I'll do it all over again, owning her over and over. I want her pussy dripping with me all night, so that she's still a mess in the morning. So much that during the day she'll suddenly be wet from my come leaving her pussy. A private remind that she's mine.

Aspen contracts around my cock and I go blind at the sensation. She's so fucking tight and hot. Being this close to her, as deep inside her as I can go, is the only thing I ever want to feel. I would fuck her until we both died if that's how we wanted to go.

"Gailen, please," she mumbles and arches her back so my pelvis hits her clit more directly. I snap my hips harder and she slaps her hands over her mouth as she screams, squeezing my cock in a rhythm that makes it hard to hold on, but I do.

As she comes down I move close to her, so that all I can see is her eyes locked on mine.

"Beg me to fill you up, bad girl. Beg for your last punishment."

"Give me your come. I want it," she whimpers, and contracts her inner muscles around me. It sets off my orgasm, and I thrust deep as I spill inside her.

"My bad fucking girl filled up with my come," I grunt as my pleasure subsides. I stay deep inside her, holding her to my body, feeling our breath match again and move our bodies like a wave.

"I didn't think I'd like being called a bad girl," she says, still breathing hard.

"I always know what my girls needs to hear," I laugh, and bite her ear.

36

Gailen

My brain and body revert back to habit now that I'm in the Sorrelle compound, even if I'm sleeping somewhere unfamiliar. I wake up at 4:30 A.M. even though Aspen and I were up enjoying each other until sometime after midnight. It's a compulsion I can't fight, so I do what I would have done without her.

I get up, I get dressed, and I go train. It's weird to move through the house to the training area instead of coming from the room I had in the staff quarters. No one else seems to be awake yet, and that somehow makes it creepy. Even when I've been on night duty, there's a different kind of silence this early in the morning.

On my way through the kitchen, I grab a banana and eat quickly.

Other guards are in the gym when I walk in. I get a couple curious looks, but no one says anything to me directly. I haven't been one of them in years, even if I know who all of them are. Alonzo was always the better choice for head of security and he hired quality men who would take care of the Sorrelles. It's not hard to be loyal to them.

Still, not only am I the guy that would go in and out of the house while on a hunt for the lost sister, now I'm back and I'm sure that it's made it to the staff that Aspen and I are together. That I slept in one of the house bedrooms last night. I'm sure they know all about the fight between the sisters. The staff always know more than anyone realizes.

They might think I'm overstepping the line, that I've crossed an ethical boundary, but they don't really know me, or know Aspen. I have to remind myself of that. It's not like I don't see it. If I wasn't the person involved, I would have concerns too. I would think less of the person in my place.

Yet I can't regret a single second. I'd endure every look or murmured insult for her.

I go through my cardio and weight routine, but don't bother sparring. It's not something I need to do right now and I don't need to present any of these guys with a chance for them to call me out. Trust me, in a measuring contest, my dick is definitely bigger, and I don't need to knock their confidence down when we need them to keep the family safe now more than ever.

Without a word, I leave the gym and move through the house. It's inconvenient to have to go so far for a shower, but I'd rather be with Aspen. She's incredibly inconvenient but I don't mind.

I'm smiling to myself with that thought when I look up and see a small shadow in the doorway of the library.

I jump, startled the unexpected apparition. Especially from that room.

Anora steps out of the shadows.

"Can we talk?"

No, I want to respond. I don't want to talk to her. Things are all good and we're moving forward and I'm fine leaving them at that. Not to mention, I haven't set foot in that room in over four years. Not since I looked inside and saw blood everywhere, saw the people that I cared about and put my life on the line for injured and dead.

Anora seems to sense my hesitation. "Please?"

"Not in there." My voice cracks and I'm ashamed.

She seems surprised, but after a moment steps away and closes the door. I follow her into the living room and we take the seats by the unlit fireplace. I sit on the edge of the chair, aware that I'm sweaty and disgusting and not wanting to get their furniture dirty. Not wanting to leave a mark of my presence on their living space. It's an ingrained habit.

"I'm sorry about yesterday."

"Are you?" I challenge. We haven't talked about it yet, but I'm guessing I'm no longer employed by the Sorrelles after yesterday's revelations. It takes the leash off some of my inner thoughts and feelings when it comes to talking to them.

Anora narrows her eyes for a second, then sighs and leans back in the chair. "No. Kind of." She laughs a little. "There's a lot to adjust to, and I jumped to the easiest reaction instead of processing what was actually bothering me."

"Which is what?"

"That I missed out on another experience with her. To get to be beside her while she has a crush and falls in love. It was hard enough to see how much she's changed and how much I missed, but then this idea that something is already going to take her away from us was a shock I wasn't ready for."

I understand what she's saying. "Even without me, she wasn't going to stay."

"I know that, too," Anora nods. "I was hoping for a visit at least when all the danger is over."

"That's a conversation to have with her, but I'm not in a rush to take her away. I'm on your side on this, Anora. You have to know that."

"I do. I do," she insists again. Her head drops and she presses her fingertips to her eyes. "I want things to be done. I want to move on."

"I can't say I saw this coming."

"We should have. We should've known she wouldn't let it go. If

Derick and Owen had killed him..."

Honestly, I'm surprised how casually Anora talks about the fact that her husband and brother-in-law should've murdered someone. Not that I disagree. I thought they were soft in that moment, especially knowing that Roger had helped Elton setup Anora's kidnapping. He knew what Elton planned to do, and didn't consider how it would come back on him. How it should have come back on him.

"We can't change the past. Let's rectify it in the future."

A hard, amused look flashes in Anora's eyes. I didn't expect it, and it reminds me once again that Anora is the most secretive member of her family. There's a whole side of her that I don't think anyone knows, maybe not even Owen. A darkness lives deep in her that she keeps caged, and I'd hate to know what it's like when it comes out. She wears a very good mask.

"We will," she says quietly, and there's a threat in it that I know isn't aimed at me. "Are we okay?"

"Even without this, we were okay. I know better than anyone how fucked up this all is. I would do anything for her, even the things she doesn't know she needs."

Anora gives me a small smile. "Good. Now go away, you smell."

I laugh and leave her in the living room with her own thoughts.

37

Aspen

Tension never entirely leaves my body. I'm braced for something and I don't even know exactly what's coming. It's exhausting.

Even Gailen sneaking me away to make me orgasm isn't enough to get me to fully relax. I sleep fitfully after he turns me into a satisfied, sweaty noodle. Even if he can make my body behave, my mind can't let it go.

It's been too fucking silent.

We know Roger is in Chicago. He's holed up in a hotel downtown, rented out the entire floor for him and his staff. He comes and goes but doesn't seem to be doing any business or preparation of any kind.

I've honestly started to wonder if he's doing all of this to fuck with us and has no intentions of following through on anything further. I'm sure he's surveilling us in return and he has to know that I'm with the Sorrelles. Maybe this is his weird version of psychological warfare because it's working.

Every unexpected sound makes me jump. When I come around a corner and run into someone I'm not expecting I flinch, sometimes I even make a sound. It's embarrassing and I can't get myself under control. I hate that.

I've been doing a lot of wandering. Even if Isaac and Aster both acknowledge my hacking skills outstrip theirs, we're operating in a world that they know more about than I do. I'm not physical risk to anyone so training isn't useful.

I've gone to the gun range a few times.

Mostly I sit with the kids. Bran, as the baby, needs someone who can hang out and keep him out of trouble. He's a good distraction, until I start fearing what will happen to the kids if something happens to their parents. Until I start wondering how I'll feel if I'm responsible for another orphan in this world.

The first time that thought really hit me I was so upset I threw up my breakfast.

Gailen held me on the floor of the bathroom even though I smelled like vomit, rocking me and whispering to me until I could hold it together again.

We're having a family dinner when Owen's phone rings. I'm surprised by how much I've accepted calling these meals that.

He glances down at the screen absentmindedly and I watch as his normally neutral, passive expression morphs into something harder. Angrier. He meets my eyes across the table and I know. I don't know how, I didn't know I could interact with any of them like that, but I know what that look is telling me.

It's Roger.

Owen answers the phone and puts it on speaker.

"Sorrelle," he answers. I love that Owen took their surname when he married Anora. It fit. With everything I know about their lives, probably more than they think, he would be part of the family regardless of his marriage.

Roger starts with a scoff. "It's Forrester."

"I'm aware." Owen's voice is like a blade, and I wonder if that's a skill I could learn. Focusing on that is stopping me from panicking.

"I know that bitch is in your house. Are you there Aspen? You better listen up."

Owen rolls his eyes, but I still get up from my chair and move to Gailen. He pushes back from the table and pulls me down onto his lap. I focus on breathing with him, and his big hand splays across my abdomen. My eyes won't relax, jumping from thing to person to thing, until I catch on Anora. She's got a small smile on her face as she watches me with Gailen.

It's been a few days and her and I still haven't talked. Not even the conversation I meant to have with her, and definitely not about Gailen and I. Seeing her reaction to the way I sought him out for comfort makes me think maybe that second conversation isn't necessary. He told me they talked, but didn't tell me details, and I didn't pry. He has a history with my family and I'm not going to change that.

"What do you want, Roger?" Owen says, sounding bored.

"You don't care about that little bastard. Give her to me, and our business with one another is concluded. Forever. I'll even sign an agreement. I will never interfere with any business related to the Sorrelle family." Which means protection for Derick and Alina, too. It's protection for the Sorrelles, Designation, and Venture. It's a good deal, especially since Roger will likely cause annoyance and disruption otherwise.

He doesn't have the power or influence anymore to destroy them, but he's got enough money to insert himself into their business and delay things. Enough money to hurt them if he was so inclined.

"And what will you do with her, if we agree?"

My stomach clenches and I immediately start sweating. I don't think Owen will agree to it, even if he should, but the statement itself still makes me sick. The idea of being betrayed again is so real, and so easy for me to believe.

"Breathe with me, baby," Gailen whispers against the back of my neck. "Focus on me. You're safe. I'm here. You're safe."

I'm never safe, but right now I'm safe enough. If they would turn on me, I could get out of here. All that wandering the last few days means I know the house well now. I know how I could get out. I know that Gailen would get me out.

"Does it matter?" Roger snarls.

"I want to know what I'd be party to, if we took your agreement."

"I'll make her pay for what she did to me, and then I'll finish what her brother started. I'll put her to work. It's the only thing she's good for."

"So you won't kill her?"

"I won't kill her, but I'll make sure she feels fucking sorry for what she did. She'll be lucky if she ever walks again. But will she really need to if I have her chained to a desk all goddamn day?" Roger huffs again. "Stop wasting my time, Carver, do we have a deal or not?"

Owen's cheeks turn pink at being called by his prior name. The name he abandoned.

"I'll get back to you." He hangs up the phone.

"So, trap or sneak attack?" Alina leans back in her chair, getting comfortable. "I vote for sneak attack."

"I vote for trap," Isaac contradicts her. "We can set the ground rules and he'll be overconfident."

"What are you talking about?" I ask, barely holding on to my panic.

Alina answers. "We can set a trap, tell him we'll trade you, and then turn on him and take them out. Or, since we know what he wants, we catch him off guard and take him out."

"What about making the trade?"

"Absolutely not!" Aro and Anora say at the same time.

"It's not even an option," Owen finishes. "It's our fault we're in this situation."

"What?" I slump against Gailen, my mind spinning with confusion.

"If I'd killed him before," Derick growls. "We wouldn't be here right now. We made you vulnerable, Aspen. He shouldn't be alive to come after you, and that was our fault."

"What?" I say again, in greater disbelief. "You aren't responsible for this."

"We all are," Anora interjects.

"We were soft because we were scared," Alina adds. "We wanted answers and got them. You wanted justice and got it. There are so many decisions we all could have made differently than could've prevented this. It's on all of us, so all of us will clean it up."

I nod, hearing her. Roger Forrester isn't only my enemy. He and Derick had animosity that went back years, before I ever did anything to Roger. Before Elton even crafted his plans to take Anora. The Sorrelles and I have the same nemesis, and the only way we can take him down is together.

"Then I vote trap."

Gailen huffs a small laugh at my back. "Of course you do."

I twist in his lap. "What about you then?"

"Let me find out who he's working with, and then I'll decide trap or sneak attack."

"Good idea. Get on that," Owen orders. He pinches the bridge of his nose and squeezes his eyes shut. "Fuck. Can't we ever have a normal dinner?"

"No, my love," Anora answers. "But we can keep trying."

It all breaks up after that, with everyone heading off in separate directions to get things done. Gailen trails me upstairs and I know before he gets to work finding out who Roger hired, he's going to try and relax me again.

I'm not going to fight him.

He closes the door to our bedroom and leans against it, staring me down. I enjoy the view - his long, muscular body in fitted denim and a tight t-shirt. His brown hair is getting long and a piece in the front falls across his forehead and into his eyes. Eyes that are stripping me down right that second, and causing my pussy to clench.

"You're being a bad girl again, Aspen."

"Am I?" I play.

"Getting all tense when you know I'd never let anything happen to you." He pushes off the door and stalks toward me. "Do you think I'd ever let anything happen to you?" Gailen wraps a hand around my throat and gently pulls me close. His mouth parts mine in a soft, wet kiss. When he pulls away I can see the strand of saliva that connects our lips and it makes me shiver.

He cocks an eyebrow. "Open your mouth."

I do as he says because I like playing this bad girl game. I like seeing what he'll do to me, now that he feels safe pressing our boundaries together.

Gailen stares at me and then opens his mouth, his tongue sliding out toward my waiting mouth. I feel rather than see the saliva drip off his tongue and onto mine, and I moan but keep my mouth open until he tells me otherwise. His mouth closes and he watches my eyes, then my mouth, before giving me a panty-melting smirk.

"Swallow."

I close my mouth and do as he says.

"Clothes off, bend over the bed."

I nearly trip in my desire to do as he says as quickly as possible. I spread my legs a little and bend over, offering myself to him. Gailen comes up behind me and pulls me back a little, then pushes me down so my head is resting on the edge of the bed. My hands nearly touch my toes.

I hear him kneel down behind me and clench when he slides a finger along my already soaking and eager pussy.

"Did you like my spit in your mouth, bad girl?"

"Yes," I answer.

"Did it make this sweet little pussy all wet?"

"Yes."

Gailen grips my ass cheeks and spreads me open. I'm not expecting what he does next.

He spits on my pussy.

His saliva is cooler than my skin, and I gasp at the shock of it. I feel it on my entrance and dripping on my pussy lips.

"Did you like that?"

"Yes," I admit.

"Such a bad girl."

Gailen is still holding onto my ass cheeks, and I feel him move. He spits again, this time right onto my asshole. I gasp even harder, my hips automatically jumping forward. I moan when he bites into my ass cheek, and his warm breath taunts all the sensitive flesh at the apex of my thighs.

I bury my face in the blankets when he licks me, starting at my clit and all the way up. He doesn't stop at my pussy, and I cry out when the point of his tongue presses into my asshole. I don't do anything but moan as he teases that entrance with his tongue. It's a feeling I can't describe, it almost tickles, but at the same time I feel like my legs are turning to liquid and I want to fall over from how good it feels.

My pussy is clenching and getting wetter by the second, and I can feel my sticky arousal dripping down my thighs.

Gailen slides two fingers into my pussy and continues to eat my ass. I work against him, fucking his fingers and his tongue, suffocating him with my ass cheeks as he eats me from behind. It feels incredible.

"Show me what a bad girl you are." His breath skates along my lower back as he encourages me. "Come, baby." I cry out when his tongue plunges firmly into my asshole and his fingers curl against my front wall. It takes seconds for me to tip over into an orgasm, squeezing around him. He moans as he feels it, the vibration tickling me in an unbelievably pleasant way that prolongs my orgasm.

"Fuck me, please," I beg as I come down. Gailen kisses my lower back and then stands. It doesn't take long for him to press his cock inside me and it nearly sends me spiraling into another orgasm. He fucks me slow, sliding his entire length in and out of me. I slump against the bed, unable to do anything except feel him.

"More, bad girl?" he asks, moving slightly faster.

"More."

"Glutton for punishment," he grunts. There's a pressure against my asshole and I relax as Gailen's thumb slides inside. His fingers splay across my lower back and dig in as he moves my body with that thumb hooked into my ass. The friction is more than I can handle, and I swear I see stars as he uses my body.

"I can feel that tight ass squeezing me, bad girl. Come for me."

I move back on him, following his push and pull.

"Gailen," I moan. "Fill me," I beg.

As the orgasm hits, my entire body clamps down, all my muscles tightening and my back arching as I scream.

"Fuck," Gailen groans and his movements get jagged and unsteady. His hips smack into mine and hold as he comes inside me.

Before I can come down, Gailen pulls out of me and presses his fingers inside my pussy again. The wet sounds of our come inside me are carnal and lascivious. He moves his fingers to my asshole and pushes inside, spreading me open.

I cry out when he uses his other hand to fuck my pussy too. I've got four fingers inside me, the loud sounds of my arousal amping up the pleasure.

"One more, bad girl. That's how I'll know you're really sorry. Apologize with your pussy and your ass, baby. Come from me playing with you like this."

"Oh god," I moan. "Gailen, please. I'm good, I promise."

"Prove it." He crooks his fingers in my pussy and I swear I explode.

I scream into the blankets but it does almost nothing to muffle the sounds of my pleasure. My lower body clenches around him and I gush around his hands, come dripping down my thighs.

When I relax, he carefully removes himself from me and helps me kneel down on the ground. He wraps himself around me and I snuggle into his neck, inhaling the scent of sharp citrus mixed with his sweat.

"I love you," I sigh out. "I really fucking love you."

"Good." Gailen kisses the top of my head, and we laugh. I feel better, and I didn't expect that at all.

38

Gailen

After making sure Aspen can stand by herself in the shower, I step out and get myself dressed. I text Isaac to get ready to do some surveillance, and he's waiting for me in the entryway when I come downstairs. He must have already been in the house when I sent the message.

Aster and Isaac hide out in the old guest house that they renovated to their specifications. I've never been inside, and according to rumor, only Owen has. They're intensely private about it and it makes me think they've got some kind of kinky sex dungeon vibe going on in there. I wouldn't put it past either of them, considering how they started.

It's amusing to me now that I ever thought I could be with Aster. I admired her, and I thought that admiration could turn into more. It was surprisingly easy to take her rejection, and that's when I knew my feelings were more in my head than grounded in reality.

Once I got to know Isaac, not only did he become my friend, I knew he was perfect for her. He offered her a level of understanding I never would have been capable of, and it helped me repair my friendship with her, too. After Aro, there's no one I trust more than them. Until Aspen, anyway.

"I'm driving," Isaac smirks at me and grabs keys from the rack by the door.

I roll my eyes. "It was one fucking time."

"But it proved that I am better at evasive driving than you and we don't know what we're about to find. The superior skill should be in charge."

I give him a shove and we get into the SUV that's waiting outside.

We don't talk as he drives to the hotel Roger is occupying, and we don't need to talk either. Both of us know what's going to happen when we get there, and even though I would consider us friends, there's not much for either of us to say. I know that he'll do what needs to be done to protect Aspen, end of story. That's all I need to know.

Isaac finds a place to park near the hotel, sets up his laptop, and starts working. We're near enough that he can get into the hotel wi-fi and access all the internal systems. While he snoops digitally, I'm on surveillance to see who is coming in and out. Roger took the top floor of the building, which is less defensible than he thinks. It tells me that he might have hired a team, but he's not listening to them.

When I was a merc, there was no way I would've let that happen. But if the client pushes back, at the end of the day the client wins. Even when it's going to get them killed.

Isaac gets into the security system and opens up the camera feeds for Roger's floor. We're watching the setup of the guards, and then someone walks out of the door of the main suite. I feel a jolt of recognition and apprehension down my spine as the large man approaches one of the guards and they start talking. It's easy to see he's pissed, and that's going to work in our favor.

"I think I have a plan," I murmur to Isaac as I pull out my phone.

"You know that guy?"

"Yeah. Give me a minute."

It takes Patrick five rings before he picks up and I'm surprised he picked up at all.

"The fuck you want?"

"You heard from Otter lately?"

Silence.

"Why?"

"The mercs on my girl's ass."

"Fuck. Want me to call him?"

"He told me to lose his number and I listened." When I decided to leave my team, it didn't go over well with the leader. He accused me of being too soft for the work they did, and he was probably right. It felt wrong to be violent for causes and people I didn't care about. Even when we were saving people in retrieval, it haunted me. I was fucking good at it but at what cost?

I think that's what really pissed Otter off. I was damn good, and in the moment I could shut down everything but my training and instincts. It was after, when I came back to myself, that it got to me. The ability to shut down was one I saw as a negative. If I was going to take a life I wanted to feel it. Choose it. Know that I was consciously taking another person's chances away.

When I went to work for the Sorrelles I was still recovering from what I had done, and it made me a bit arrogant and a bit sloppy. Alina putting her trust in me to lead security when she left was more than I was ready for, and I wish I'd been smart enough to turn her down. Losing Don put me in a tailspin I didn't know how to recover from.

Now, I can acknowledge my skills, but more than anything I want to use them to protect the people that matter. I still act on training and instinct, but I am fully present when I do what needs to be done, and I do it for people that deserve my defense. That's what I've been doing for years now. I protect Aspen. I protect her family. I'll never regret what I learned, I just wish I'd figured out sooner that being a mercenary wasn't for me.

"Let him know we'll pay better and Forrester will disappear so he can't talk shit."

"You sure?"

"His breaths are fucking numbered."

Patrick laughs. "Got it."

I get off the phone and Isaac is waiting expectantly for me to explain myself.

"I joined a mercenary team out of high school. They trained me, used me, and then I left."

"The team inside?"

"My old crew."

"Fuck. How screwed are we?"

"Screwed if this doesn't work. Let's go back. There's nothing more we need to know until I hear back from Patrick."

"Dinah's Patrick?"

"If either of them heard you say that, you'd get kicked in the dick." They are both very adamant about the platonic and business nature of their relationship. Her father, prior to binding her to Seamus, had plans to make them into something more. Neither of them wanted it, and if they'd been forced to follow through, would've killed each other within 48 hours. They work together well, and he never lets anyone question a woman being in the place of power she occupies, but they'd be the worst romantic relationship in history.

Isaac laughs but starts the SUV and pulls into traffic to head back to the compound.

"We can set a very different trap if I can get them to turn."

"Are they likely to?"

"Based on that footage, Otter is irritated with Roger. That works in our favor because he's not afraid to ditch a client who won't listen. It's if he's willing to turn on the client that's the question."

"How much is Roger paying them?"

I tell Isaac what were paid when I was part of the team, and that was over 6 years ago. He lets out a low whistle. "It's at least double that now, I'd guess."

I let out a murmur of agreement. "The Sorrelles can pay it. The thing is, you don't hire them, they accept you as a client and the agreement is that they make the decisions required to accomplish your mission. You do not not micromanage the team. Roger Forrester is the client of their nightmares. He must have had a hell of a referral."

"How come I've never heard of them? Clive knows everyone."

"Clive knows them. But even he knows what secrets to keep. He'd make a referral if it was needed."

Isaac's eyebrows shoot up toward his forehead and I can watch as his brain processes and rewrites his vision of me. I might not long for the kill and seek it out like he and Aster do, but I am capable of violence. If we'd compare body counts, I don't think we'd be as far apart as he might have believed before.

I kill for protection. They kill for vengeance. We're two sides of the same coin.

"How long?"

"Four years." I sigh. "Might as well be forty in that life. It never stops. There's no time off, no vacations. It's mission, prep, rinse, repeat."

"We had no idea."

"Until Aspen, Alina was the only one who knew. I'm assuming she told Don, maybe Owen, but I think she picked up on my shame before I could express it."

"You did what you had to do to survive."

"Maybe," I hedge, not willing to agree or disagree with that statement. Yes, I needed a way out and a skill. I ended up being a natural at taking lives. But I will always wonder what would've happened if I'd taken another path, even if I know this is the one that led me to Aspen.

I can protect her because of that choice, and that makes it an easier pill to swallow.

The fact that watching me kill for her gets her worked up is a side benefit.

I thought she'd be afraid of me, hesitant of me, but instead she rips my clothes off.

Fuck, I love her.

"So you and Aspen."

I facepalm. "Really, dude?"

Isaac laughs. "Nah, her and I had a good talk. Sorrelle magic. Fate."

"I'm her soulmate, huh?"

"No doubt. You were always different than the other guards, always more, and now we know why. You were meant to be family."

"You're gonna make me fucking cry," I tease, even though what he said heals a fissure inside me that I hadn't know was still open. That they always saw me differently, and that they'll accept me. For myself, and not only because of Aspen.

I'll keep proving to them I'm worthy of it.

39

Aspen

Gailen is anxious when he and Isaac get back, and he puts me off saying it'll be easier to tell everyone at once. There's a look that passes between him and Isaac that makes me feel like he's keeping secrets, and it makes me paranoid. Did they change their minds? Am I really safe here?

It's late, so he convinces me that we'll talk about it all in the morning. That does nothing to help me sleep.

I roll over and look at him in the dark, and do what I do best - I analyze.

Everything he's shared with me, promised me, revealed to me. Every expression, even the relaxed look of his body and face in deep sleep. I've felt the tension in his body, been aware of it almost as if it were my own.

Both nights we slept in motels, his body was tense even when he was sleeping. He didn't trust his surroundings and he didn't trust me.

Now, he is as relaxed and deeply blissed out into sleep as it's possible to be. Gailen feels safe. Not only here at the compound, but beside me. That level of trust from someone like him is a gift, and I know because earning my trust is just as difficult. Gailen has earned it, and I need to remind myself of all the ways he accomplished that feat.

He always stood up for me, what I wanted, prioritized what I needed, and listened to what I asked for even when he disagreed with me. Gailen made sure I always had an out, and that I knew he always had my back.

Whatever happened tonight has shaken him, but it didn't take him away from me. It didn't betray my trust. I can step back from the ledge and trust.

With that thought repeating in my head like a mantra, I fall asleep beside him.

I wake up to Gailen's fingers trailing up and down my spine.

"I changed my mind."

"About what?" I murmur sleepily.

"Waiting. I need to tell you."

"Okay." I try to turn over but he stops me.

"Like this, please." The pain in his voice makes my heart ache, and I already know there's nothing he could say to me right now that will change how I feel about him. This is the moment I'll prove that to him.

"You know I was a mercenary." I nod. "I just…I killed a lot of people, and some of them didn't deserve it. I killed for money, not loyalty or anyone's safety, or because it was the right thing to do. Sometimes it was, but that was incidental. It wasn't even part of the job to protect the team - if someone fell, we left them. It was…I didn't feel it at the time. I didn't let myself. All I wanted was a purpose.

"Then there was a job…a friend died right next to me. His brain was on my face. It was the thing that woke me up. I left, and I didn't leave my team on good terms. The other dregs like me, we were fine, but my team leader was pissed. He let me go but he's good at holding grudges. Alina hired me and I tried to accept who I had been and figure out who I wanted to be. I don't think I knew until I started hunting you."

"You're welcome," I snark, and feel relieved when he laughs. "Why are you telling me this now?"

"I needed you to know the whole truth because this might go wrong and it might be my fault."

"What?" Now I roll over to face him and he doesn't stop me this time. I cup his cheek in my hand and he closes his eyes.

"Roger hired my old team." The sound of his voice borders on agony. "I'm trying to reach out and I think it will work, but I could also see Otter doubling down to fuck me over."

"Then we'll find another way. But even if this Otter person decides to be a petty little bitch, it won't be your fault."

"Sure," he answers with a frown.

"Why Otter?"

"He was a SEAL. But when he first joined the Navy the dude was a tall string bean. He went all in with training and bulked up hard in order to qualify for SEALS. Fucking huge. But that image of the tall skinny guy in the water stuck. Like an otter."

I laugh. "Did you have a nickname?"

Gailen is quiet, his cheeks a little pink. I love it when he blushes.

"Bloodhound."

I laugh so hard my stomach hurts, and he rolls me over and slides between my legs. He pulls my wrists over my head and holds me down.

"Think that's funny?"

"Hilarious. Perfect." I stop laughing to stare up into his eyes. "You're perfect."

"Far from it, baby, but I'll let you have your delusions." Then he kisses me until I can't think anymore about anything except the way he makes me feel.

40

Gailen

Patrick picks me up at the Sorrelle compound. He was cagey even for him on the phone but he's also one of the most paranoid people I know. Especially when it comes to our old team. It's why his code name was Phillip, after the author Phillip K. Dick. Always paranoid, always doubting intentions, always sure that someone is out to get him.

We're meeting with Otter in the middle of a turbine field a few hours away. It's out in the open where sight lines fuck all of us, but we'll see anything coming. I'm surprised Roger let Otter out of his sight, given that he's obsessively monitored everything the man does. Isaac and Aster kept tabs on the hotel hall, and Roger called for him at all hours.

I couldn't tell if Roger was also paranoid, or if he liked lording his power over a man who could break his neck with a pinky finger. Most likely it's a combination of both.

"Did he say he'd take the deal?"

"No. He wanted to see you."

"Fuck."

"It could go either way," Patrick tries to reassure me in a bland voice. "Maybe he wants to apologize. The guys didn't like how he dismissed you." He turns onto the gravel road that will lead us to the meeting. "Others left, after you. It shook some of their confidence in him. So he could be mad at you about that or our charismatic leader could be ready to acknowledge that he screwed up."

It's the most I've heard him say consecutively while sober.

"Who left?"

"Traitor, GI Joe, and Cowboy."

"Cowboy had to hurt."

"I think that was the one that made him see the light."

Otter is already in the location, leaning against the hood of his SUV. He's all in black, wearing more than one gun on his person, and his arms across over his burly chest. Even under his black baseball cap I can see threads of silver in his hair. It's been six years but my mentor and trainer has definitely aged. It's what this work does to you.

Patrick parks and we both get out of the car. We aren't hiding that we're armed either, and if we tried I think Otter would rip us to pieces. There's no reason to conceal anything. Not with the kind of ask I'm making. It wouldn't be hard for Otter to kill us both and it would be quite some time before anyone found the bodies. We're good but Otter is the best.

"I'm not turning," Otter starts before we say anything else. "But I might be willing to quit."

"For a price?"

"For information. You know I don't look into things more than I have to, so what the hell makes this Aspen girl so fucking special? What the hell did she do?"

I glance over at Patrick and he shakes his head slightly - he didn't tell Otter about my relationship with Aspen. As far as Otter knows, this is only because I work for the Sorrelles.

Otter might not go looking for information, but he won't look away from it when he comes across it. I hesitate for a second and then let the entire Sorrelle saga spill out of my mouth. The highlights, the big events, even some of the small details.

The incidental murder of Benjamin Forrester nee Lassiter and how it led to the murder of Don Sorrelle, Roger's obsessive nephew Elton, how he abused Aspen, and used her to help him kidnap Anora. How Aspen got revenge by ruining Roger's quest for political power. Leaving him rich but impotent.

Otter laughs at that. He grew up abused and bullied so I know hearing Aspen's story will speak to him, even if he tries to pretend he exists without emotions. She's scrappy, fought for herself, and built something without anyone's help. Minimally, he'll respect her.

"I think I'm in love."

Patrick snorts and looks away.

Otter looks at me, and shakes his head. "I guess I'm too late. That's your girl?"

"Yeah."

He nods. "I get why you'd take the risk to meet me."

"So what are you going to do?"

"I don't know."

"The Sorrelles are good people to know," I offer.

"I'm sure," he sighs. "But this sounds like a war I don't want to be in the middle of, Bloodhound. I'm just here to do a job."

I'm disappointed but not surprised. He hasn't killed me, so the conversation was at least worth having.

"You good, kid?" Otter asks, catching me off guard.

"Better than ever." It's true. The healing I've done, the things I've learned about myself, and all of it leading to the woman who is the reason I breathe…yeah, I'm pretty fucking great.

"Good to know. I was a dick."

"Yeah."

"Right."

Patrick and I back up around our vehicle, not turning our backs on Otter even if this has been good meeting and I don't think he'd take us out. Otter resumes his stance with crossed arms and leaning against the hood of his car. He watches us back up and drive off without moving. Without even appearing to breathe. He'll probably stand there for at least half an hour to make sure we're not turning on him.

"What are you going to do?"

"No fucking clue. Point and pray?"

Patrick scoffs at me and picks up his phone to make a call. "Boss? Rally the troops."

"Thanks," I say softly when he hangs up.

"Seriously, don't mention it."

We ride the rest of the way to the Sorrelle compound in silence.

41

Aspen

Gailen looks defeated when he gets back.

We pile inside the library, which only seems to darken his expression further.

It's one of the rooms in this place I haven't gone inside yet.

I know what it looked like when Don was murdered. Elton made me look at the confirmation photos that the job was done. He made me look at my father's dead body.

That's all I can see now. Every blink, the red pool of blood flashes behind my eyes.

Gailen tenses too. We stand close together as if bracing ourselves for the room to hit us. It does, in a way. I take his hand in mine and squeeze.

It looks different now. They still call it the library but it isn't one anymore. The room is painted in soft colors and there's squishy furniture everywhere, as well as a little fenced off play area. They repurposed this room for something happy. If the ghost of Don Sorrelle haunts this place, at least his ghost is with his grandchildren.

Anora is watching me, but I look away.

She knows.

This room is going to eat me alive until we get out. This is the room where my biggest guilt lives. The thing I can't forgive myself for, even if I did it under duress and Elton's demand. Don is dead because of me. The blood that soaks this room is because of me.

"It's still habit to come in here," Gailen says softly to me. "It still feels like the center of the house even when we pretend it's not."

Owen clears his throat and looks at Gailen expectantly.

"He didn't accept or reject the offer. He took in information. It's wait and see."

"Then trap it is," Alina steps up, her shoulders thrown back like she's ready to step into battle right that second. "Set up the meet, take him out."

"Patrick rallied Dinah and the Rileys, probably the Brennans too, if we want it."

"No," Aster disagrees. "We keep it small. We make him believe we're making the trade."

"Excuse me, don't I have a say here?" I step into the center. "Since I'm the bait."

"What do you want to do?" Alina asks.

"Be the bait."

"No," Gailen says forcefully and steps up to me. He pulls me close and presses his forehead to mine. "I can't take that risk."

"It's not yours to take, and I'm not asking permission," I answer.

"Aspen." His eyes squeeze shut. "If anything happens to you, I will lock you up and never let you leave ever again."

If anyone but him said that to me, it would cause me to panic. With Gailen, I would gladly let him keep me captive.

"When this is over, we're going to do that anyway. You and me and the rest of our lives." Tears spring to my eyes and I squeeze them shut to hold them in.

"Don't make me puke," Aster groans.

"Says the one with a public sex kink," I drawl back as I pull away from Gailen to a socially acceptable distance.

"Children, please," Aro jokes. "It's time to make a plan."

42

Aspen

Owen and Roger arranged a meeting place, date, and time.

We basically agreed to whatever Roger wanted because based on what Gailen learned, he was making decisions based on ego and arrogance rather than the skill of his team. This was confirmed when he picked the top floor of a parking garage in the middle of the city. It's barely defensible and leaves everyone open to snipers. Historically, the merc crew had one and at least one backup.

I'm scared but I want this done.

I am putting my very limited trust in this family that I resisted being part of for years. They tried to be a hand that fed me and I bit them. Repeatedly. Pushed them away over and over.

Yet here they are, taking a stand for me, and for themselves. Our enemy is the same and we are stronger together.

While I still don't think they understand me, I'm starting to believe they are open to trying. That when I'm ready to speak, they'll hear me. Maybe I do have a future as part of this family, even if it's not something expected or traditional.

Since everyone outside the family has the impression that Owen is an ice king, he's the one that will be standing next to me during the trade. It will appear as if it's the two of us and the head guard, Alonzo, and his backup, Gailen. There was no way I was going to face Roger without him by my side, and we both agreed on that point.

We're hoping that such a small group of us will lure Roger into a false sense of strength. That he won't think about where everyone else is.

Anora is staying with the kids. She wasn't a fan of that but did acknowledge that she's not much use outside being a crack shot. It's the kind of protection that might be necessary if we find that Roger is a liar.

Owen drives, Alonzo is in the passenger seat, and I'm in the back feeling a little too much like a prisoner transport for comfort, even with Gailen next to me. I feel vulnerable as fuck.

Gailen reminded me, repeatedly, that it's going to be okay and I can trust them.

He trusts them, and they've earned at least a medium amount of trust from me, too.

All the trust in the world won't stop my racing heart and the thoughts that this might go wrong. Gailen probably didn't realize he gave me enough information to find out who Otter really is and his history. Information usually makes me feel calmer. In this case, it did not.

I doubt even Gailen really knows Otter. How dangerous and intelligent he is.

We have no idea what we're walking into, and we might be in over our heads.

The mercenary team is spread out around the floor, ranged around a silver sedan. We pull up and wait in our car. The tension has a scent - it's sharp and anticipatory. Almost sour. It does not help my queasy feelings.

Otter walks forward and beckons to us to get out of the car.

Gailen and Alonzo get out first, making a show of surveying the situation, before they come around to the other side and open the doors for Owen and I. Owen takes the lead, and I cower behind him. Gailen takes a firm grip on my upper arm, and I make an obvious struggle, like I'm trying to pull away.

We walk to the front of our car but remain distant. There's at least 20 feet between us.

Roger exits the back of the sedan. He looks like shit. His hair is pure white and thin, combed over his head to try and cover where it's gotten patchy. He's somehow chubby and thin at the same time, his suit ill-fitting because it's baggy in the chest and shoulders but barely fits around his paunch of a belly. Like it's all coalescing right there, while everything else has been eaten away.

I want to feel bad because he is technically my uncle, but he let his sister be abused and then murdered by her son. He let me be abused. I know that even outside of what he did to us, Roger Forrester is a parasite of a human being and he's responsible for a lot of harm and death even if he didn't pull the trigger himself.

The sneer on his face doesn't scare me. I glare back at him as our eyes meet.

"Bring her to me."

Nobody moves.

"We haven't signed the agreement. I want it in writing she won't be killed, and I need you to understand what we will be obligated to do if that's ignored. She might not be family but she's blood, and you can't disrespect our blood." The ice in Owen's voice makes my spine stiffen, even if he warned me this is what he was going to say.

"She's my blood, too. I won't kill her. You have my word."

Owen steps forward and slides his hands into his pockets, oozing arrogant command.

"When have you ever given me a reason to trust your word, Roger? Get the fucking contract," Owen bites out.

Roger stares, then signals to someone behind him. A weaselly guy in a suit gets out of the back of the sedan with a briefcase, and fumbles and stumbles as he moves toward his boss. He slides a stack of papers out and holds them out for Roger.

"Give them to him, imbecile."

The man runs over, crossing the no man's land between us. He doesn't seem to realize the precarious position until he's about halfway across, and then moves even faster which somehow makes him even clumsier.

He holds out the papers to Owen. For fun, Owen stares him down for a moment before taking the papers. Owen reads them carefully, and the rest of us watch Roger's assistant scramble back to his side of the confrontation.

Owen slides his hand in his jacket pocket, and the sound of safety's coming off echoes.

"I'm getting a pen, calm the fuck down." He removes a pen from his inner pocket and puts the papers on the hood. He flips through and makes adjustments, and then holds the papers out to Roger.

The assistant does the run again. This is turning from tense to humorous, and if I didn't know what was coming I'd think that it was anti-climactic. The strategy to lull Roger into frustration is working. I can tell because he's getting redder with every minute that passes.

Roger reviews the changes that Owen made and nearly turns purple.

"Fine," he snarls. I don't know what Owen added but I almost laugh. Gailen squeezes my bicep, sensing that I might be losing it. Is this hysteria? This might be hysteria.

Roger signs the papers, the assistant runs them back. Owen feigns signing, and then nods to Gailen. We start walking across the space.

We stop halfway.

"What's this?" Roger grunts.

Aster steps from the shadows, almost behind him. Roger has to turn to look at her.

The door behind us opens and bodies spill onto the rooftop. It's a mix of Sorrelle guards, and Patrick leading soldiers from the Rileys. They're all obviously armed and geared up, putting on the show that they're ready for war. Gailen and I don't move.

"Did you really think they'd let you have me?" It's my turn to speak, and I will make sure he listens to every word. "You don't matter, Roger, I made sure of it. You're not my family. You never were. They are."

"Get her!" Roger orders.

Otter steps forward and I brace myself. He looks down his nose at Roger.

"Get her yourself."

With the Rileys helping, the mercs are outnumbered even if they are more skilled than the men assembled. However, this is the kind of scenario where numbers matter. There aren't a lot of places to take cover and get defensive. Otter has to choose between the job and his men, and this time, he's choosing his man.

"Hold!" Otter shouts to his team. Roger fumes, turning around and looking at the mercs. They've still got their arms up and prepped, but the chances of them shooting are low.

Roger splutters and turns around in circles, as if something on this roof might present an answer.

"You can leave and never approach us again, or you can die." Owen shouts across the space. "You might not have your dignity, but I'll let you keep your life. Leave."

Roger roars and of all things charges at Otter.

It catches the giant off guard and gives Roger a moment to grab his sidearm. He cocks the gun and aims it at us.

Without thinking, I step in front of Gailen, blocking him as best I can.

Roger pulls the trigger.

There isn't time for anyone to do anything else.

First, I feel the force of the bullet hitting me, and it throws me back into Gailen's body. Then I feel the burn that starts in my chest and spreads like a wildfire. I smell gunpowder and copper. I taste blood in my mouth.

I hear a grunt behind me as Gailen and I fall to the ground.

There's another bang and it's so loud my ears hurt and ring. My entire head is ringing, actually. The sound of a body slumping down is dim and far away.

I think someone is saying my name.

43

Gailen

There might be chaos in my head but there's nothing but strict order happening around me. Aspen is in my arms, unconscious, and Owen and Alonzo are barking orders.

Patrick comes into view. "Give her to me. Come on."

He lifts Aspen from my arms and if it was anyone but him I'd fight him. I follow him in a daze, my own blood dripping from my arm and down the palm of my hand. It almost tickles. Aspen's blood stains my shirt.

Owen and Otter are talking, and Otter is agreeing to something. It's the last of them I see before following Patrick and a Riley soldier down a flight of stairs and out onto the next level down. We slide into an SUV. Patrick puts Aspen in my lap and then crouches next to us to work on her.

The soldier drives like the devil himself is chasing us.

I follow Patrick's instructions, and keep Aspen stable until we can get to the ER. There's a trickle of blood leaving the corner of her mouth, and her breathing sounds wrong.

She took a bullet for me.

What the fuck.

There's a team with a gurney waiting when we drive up, and they take Aspen from me before I can say anything else. Patrick answers their questions and then drags me to the waiting room.

A few minutes later, Aro, Alina, and Derick arrive. He tosses me a bag with clean clothes and I move to change my shirt. I hiss when my sleeve pulls at the graze on my arm. I ignore it.

Patrick leaves, and I get my clothes changed.

We wait. It could be all night until we know more.

After an hour, Derick moves to sit next to me. "Alina took a bullet for me."

"I know."

"I've never been angrier in my life."

"I'm not angry."

He nods but the expression on his face says he doesn't believe me. Maybe he's right. I have no idea what my feelings are well enough to articulate them. "I've also never been more terrified. She loved me enough to do that, and it was a violent reminder how easily I could lose her."

"I'm not losing her."

"Fucking right, you're not. Just don't be mad at her. Take it as a sign of what she feels for you. That she would give up all that she is for you."

"Fuck." I only love the idea that she'd die for me as a theoretical truth. The reality is the worst I've ever felt in my life. I'd burn in that cabin again and again to not have to feel the way that I do right now.

"Pretty much." He gets up and goes back to sit next to Alina, and they continue playing musical chairs because Aro comes to sit with me next.

She doesn't say anything. Being married to Harp means mastering the art of full, communicative silences. Aro's silence tells me everything I need to hear. She takes my hand in both of hers, offering me comfort, and we wait again.

Anora and Own come into the waiting room after a little under 5 hours. Since they were the last people on record with any right to Aspen as her next of kin, the doctors gave them authority over her care until she regained consciousness.

"She's going to be fine," Anora says on an exhale, her own relief palpable.

I crash forward, my face in my hands, and try to stop myself from crying in relief. I listen as Anora fills me in on what happened and that surgery was quick and went well. Aspen is going to be okay. I swallow and pull myself together.

"I am so sorry," I stand up and approach them.

Anora looks confused and Owen shakes his head in disappointment.

"For what?" Anora asks, genuinely bewildered.

"I failed to protect her."

Anora and Alina share a look, and Alina shrugs.

"Gailen, you shouldn't have been on that rooftop. We should've known if things went bad, this was a possibility. We didn't think. I'm sorry, we're sorry," Owen says in his calm, measured way.

My head is spinning. They're apologizing to me. I don't understand. "What?"

"Aspen's biggest vulnerability was you. Of course she protected you before she'd protect herself." Anora's voice is quiet and gentle, like she's trying to soothe a panicked animal. Which is not entirely inaccurate. My heart is racing and my brain is melting.

"It could've gone either way, really," Alina sighs. "It could be you in there instead."

"It should be."

"No." Anora's voice is quiet, but harsh. "You have given enough for this family. I cannot handle another piece of you on my soul."

I try to think of something to say but my mouth just gapes. It never occurred to me that they hurt for me. That Anora took what happened to me onto herself in any way. It doesn't make any sense.

"Whatever debt you think you owe, it's paid." Owen stares me down until I nod at him. "Move forward from all of this and make a life with her. She's family."

"And so are you." Aster steps into the room, Isaac a step behind her, as she finishes Owen's sentence. "Not that you've figured that out." Aspen arches a brow at me and then turns to Owen. "The body is handled."

When I'd caught Aspen, Alonzo had done is job and protected us all by shooting Roger. He'd gone down in a blast of blood and brain. I could only watch for a second before my focus returned to Aspen.

"What about the crew?" I ask. Knowing that Aspen will be fine and Roger is dead, my two biggest concerns are handled. Now I can start thinking strategically again.

"All good," Isaac says. "Patrick and the big guy spoke, shook hands, and they cleared out. I have a feeling they'll be in touch to talk about what kind of secret we're going to keep."

He was probably right. Otter had no way to contact me that I knew of, but he could get to me through Patrick. I'd be waiting for his call. Maybe this bridge wasn't as burned as I thought. Strange that this was my redemption on more that one level.

A nurse steps into the room. "She's awake and asking for Gailen."

I stand and nod at everyone, checking out of this conversation because the only thing that matters is seeing my girl. The nurse leads me through a door and down a hall. I note the two turns we take, other exits should it be necessary, and Aspen's room number. I text it to Isaac so he has it and can tell the others.

Aspen is laying in a hospital bed, looking completely fine.

I was definitely expecting a pale, barely conscious version of her. Instead, her color is good, her hair is braided over one shoulder, and she's smiling when I walk in. The bullet didn't hit anything vital, and we responded so quickly she didn't lose too much blood. She's like a cat with all her lives, but I hope this is the last one she ever loses.

As I stare at her, her smile falters.

"I got shot, you're not allowed to be mad at me," she tosses out.

I cross the room quickly and nearly collapse onto her lap. When Aspen's hands dig into my hair, I nearly lose my mind.

"Don't ever do that to me again."

She huffs a laugh. "I don't ever plan on being in a situation that would merit it. Ever again. No more danger. Can you live with that?"

I look up at her. "God, yes. When you're healed I'm stealing you away and we're not going to do anything except fuck and eat."

"Yes," she nods, and tears fill her eyes. "I'm sorry." Aspen's voice breaks and she closes her eyes, letting twin tears track down her cheeks. "His intent was me but I know he can't shoot for shit and I was sure if I did nothing he'd hit you."

I stand up and lean over so I can bring her mouth to mine. "You were a very bad fucking girl, Aspen, and I can't wait to punish you with my gratitude. Thank you, baby, for saving my life. I was furious and scared, but also in complete awe."

My hands are shaking when I take her face between them so she can't look away. "I have never loved anyone the way I love you, and experiencing proof that you feel the same way…" I break off, unable to finish my thought.

Aspen lifts her hands and places them over mine. "I love you, too. I think you're the only person I've ever loved in my life. The only person who has ever earned it, been worthy of it. Saying I would do anything for you seems weak compared to how I feel."

"Fucking hell, your punishment is getting worse and worse."

Aspen grins at me. "I can't wait."

I kiss her nose and then let her face go, but shift so our hands are entwined.

"I don't want to be the only person you love," I tell her honestly. "I want you to give your family a chance. I want you to stop being afraid."

"You're right," she nods. "I think I need to go back to therapy."

"Whatever you think will help. Do you want to see them?"

"All at once?"

I laugh. "No. We can start wherever you want."

Aspen swallows thickly and nods. "You'll stay?"

"Forever."

44

Epilogue - Gailen

6 Weeks Later

Aspen waits for her punishment. She's kneeling with her hands tied behind her back, and bent forward with her cheek resting on the floor. She's completely naked.

While she was bored and recovering, I had her do some research and tell me what aroused her. What she wanted me to do to her. It kept both of us incredibly horny all the time but also opened up conversations about needs and intimacy. We already know so much about each other that this avenue of learning has been enjoyable for both of us. She knows my mind, heart, soul, and I know the same about her.

It's been a very interesting experience to have the freedom to explore each other's bodies and desires.

As soon as the doctor cleared her, I made good on my promise and whisked her a way to a cabin in the middle of nowhere. It's on the coast of Lake Superior. I rented it for a week. No one will hear either of us scream.

I kneel down next to Aspen's side and run my fingertips down her spine, grinning as goosebumps break out across her soft skin. I squeeze her ass.

"What a nice apology," I murmur to her. "But it won't stop your punishment."

I smack her ass, but hold back from giving it the force she likes. Aspen whines, begging without words, and shifts on her knees.

"Do you like your punishments, bad girl?"

"Yes."

"Do you want this one?"

"So bad," she whines. "Please."

The please undoes me, as always, and I start spanking her in earnest. The pinker her ass cheeks get, the harder my cock grows, until it's throbbing painfully in my boxers, desperate to feel her. I slide my fingers through her slit and find her drenched.

"Have you earned my cock, bad girl?"

"No."

"That's right." I give her hands a light tug and she sits up, moving until she's comfortable. Still on her knees, ass resting on her heels, with her legs spread open. When I stand and look down at her, I can see how wet her bare pussy is for me. By the time I'm done, there's going to be a puddle of her come on the floor.

I kneel in front of her and grab her chin, kissing her with deep wet strokes of my tongue. I pull away and her eyes focus on the string of saliva that connects us. I do that repeatedly until she's shaking with arousal. Aspen's tongue is a direct line to her pussy, and it amazed me how soaked deep, wet kissing made her. She also liked my spit. In her mouth, on her nipples, dripped or expelled onto her pussy and ass. It always heightened everything for her.

Her eyes are dazed, and as I stand up she opens her mouth for me, ready to be a very good girl.

I slide off my boxers and kick them away. My dick springs free and she leans forward without prompting to take it into her mouth. I hold her hair and work her on my cock the way she likes. Not so deep that she gags, but relentless enough that it's hard for her to swallow. Aspen moans as she drools all over my cock, her chin shiny from her own spit. It makes my cock slick and drips onto my balls.

It feels so good, and she looks up to watch me as her pretty lips wrap around me. We also learned together that the sensitivity of her tongue also plays into her love of my cock in her mouth. It's another way to stimulate her.

I pull out of her mouth and step away. There's drips of spit on her naked body and a few on the floor, but it's nothing compared to the wet pool below her pussy.

"Bad, bad girl," I shake my head.

I help Aspen stand up, and kiss her as I move her toward the bed. I tweak and toy with her nipples, and she moans into my mouth. When the back of her legs hit the bed she falls down onto her back. I slide her up the bed and move over her.

"How do you want to apologize to me?" I whisper against her mouth.

"With your come inside me," she gasps as she rolls her hips, seeking me.

"That's a good girl."

I line my cock up and slide inside her to the hilt. Aspen cries out and clamps down around me, so sensitive and worked up she comes immediately. I stay still as she grinds her hips up and down, my eyes rolling into the back of my head at the tight, hot sensation of her fucking me from the bottom. I reach under her and pull on the tie binding her hands so they're free.

Immediately she wraps them around my neck and pulls me to her. We kiss as I start to roll my hips, staying as deep inside her as I can while also giving her the friction she craves. It feels incredible, and I know I won't last long either.

"What do you want, bad girl?"

"I want your come. Please come inside," she gasps, and we work against each other faster, our bodies slapping into one another as we chase release and the pleasure we love giving each other.

"You're going to make me come," I groan. "But I need to feel you first, bad girl. Show me you want it."

"I want it," Aspen cries and her movements become short and quick, and then she squeezes my cock so hard I see stars. I pound into her as she orgasms, and push deep as my own overtakes me. All I can feel is where my body touches hers, where it presses deep inside her, the way our chests press together as we breathe. It feels like I come forever, pulse after pulse filling her tight, clenching pussy.

"Yes," she murmurs as our bodies melt into each other. "So fucking good."

I slide out of her and roll to the side, but we're not done. I reach between her legs and start playing with her, sliding my fingers inside her pussy to take our come and play with her clit. She groans but rolls her hips, working with me. Two of my fingers slide back into her cunt, and the wet, obscene sound has her crying out. I sit up on my elbow and lean over to suck on one of her nipples as I continue to fuck her with my fingers.

"Listen to that…that's what happens to bad girls."

"Yes," she nods in agreement.

"Does my bad girl want more?"

"Please," she whimpers, and I press the heel of my hand into her clit. Aspen rocks her hips and comes again, squeezing my fingers and barely making a sound as she tightens up. Watching her lose it like that has me hard all over again. I can never get enough of her.

"More?" I ask.

Aspen opens her eyes and looks at me, full of fire and love.

"More."

I move back between her legs and back inside her. I start to fuck her again slowly, making her hear every wet stroke. We will never get enough of each other.

45

Epilogue - Aspen

3 Years Later

My laptop is open on the bathroom counter.

It should be weird that my sisters just listened to me pee on a stick, but it's not.

I was so anxious that I couldn't do it alone, and they would never have let me. The second I called Anora and told her I thought I was pregnant, she pulled together the video meet up. They all wait with me for the minutes to pass for the results.

On the screen, I see my face alongside their faces. The similarities that used to be so jarring are comforting now. I see pieces of myself in all of them, and that extends beyond our physical appearances too.

I did what Gailen asked - I made myself open up to loving them.

It took time, especially with Anora, but some of that was more about her than it was about me. Elton left a wound in both of us, one that might never entirely heal, but she finally understood that some of the way I am is just who I am, not as a result of how I was raised. It wasn't something to be fixed, or that needed fixing. Aster helped her see that.

Like Aster, I prefer to withdraw from people, and like Aro, I prefer to be off in my own world. Anora had to accept that distance was where I was comfortable, but it didn't mean I was closed off.

It didn't take long for all of us to bond and build individual relationships. It shocked me how easy it was to let them in, to rely on them. To feel and believe that they are my sisters. That their partners are my brothers. Their children are my nieces and nephews. That I am part of something big and full of complicated, messy love. That I belong there.

If you'd told 15 year old me that someday I'd fully be a Sorrelle, I'd have said you were fucking crazy. That I'd get a lobotomy before I let that happen.

Except it happened. Official name change and everything.

"I just want to ask the blunt question: do you want to be pregnant?" Aster interrupts my thoughts.

"It's sooner than I wanted, but yes," I nod, taking her question as it was meant.

"You're only 22," Alina adds.

"Yeah, but what will a baby change for us? Not a thing." Gailen and I both agreed we wanted kids, but we'd never really talked about a timeline for it.

"That's true," Aro agrees. "You might have to back off work for a bit though. Actually get some sleep for once in your life."

"How dare you accuse me of needing sleep." We all laugh. I'm notorious for sending messages to the group chat at all hours because when my mind starts going, I get up and I work. I also don't always pay attention to the time. At first, it was really hard on them because middle of the night texts usually meant emergencies, but I think I got them to relax in that sense as well. At least when they see the texts are from me.

"Will you stay in Wyoming?" Aro asks.

"Yeah. The renovations on the house were made with our future family in mind."

"You're not married," Anora interjects. "So if you are pregnant, we should fix that. Make sure that Gailen has legal standing to take care of you and the baby."

"You're a nerd." Aster rolls her eyes.

The timer on my phone goes off. I'm scared, I'm thrilled, I want it to be a positive test. I didn't think I'd want kids this young but I already know that if this is negative, I'm going to be sad. Not heartbroken, but definitely disappointed. The moment of clarity that I wanted this baby when I realized my period was late rocked me. I wanted to be pregnant. If I am, I want this baby without a doubt.

I needed my sisters. They'd be whatever I needed them to be, whatever the results were. The fact that I have that kind of support and stability staggers me. Little me would think it was a dream.

I grab the stick on the counter and turn it over. There's a plus in the little window.

"I'm pregnant," I whisper, tears immediately cascading down my face. I jump up from my spot on the toilet and jump around. "I'm pregnant!"

A tinny chorus of cheers and congratulations come from my laptop speaker and I move in front of the camera to show them the positive sign. The line is strong, making it pretty definitively positive.

I collapse back onto the toilet, overwhelmed with delight.

"What do I do now?" I ask.

Other than Aster, the women on the screen are mothers many times over. Aro had one more baby, a little girl named Sienna. Aro didn't know it then, but she was pregnant when we left her house all those years ago. I think Troy knew. I never did get my dog back, but it felt like he was with me to find them. Now we have a cat named Snickerdoodle and she's obsessed with Gailen.

I think she's going to do great with a baby. There's nothing she loves more than guarding things.

"Tell Gailen, figure out when it happened, make a doctor's appointment. Most won't see you until after the 8 week point," Anora answers.

"Do something cute," Aro pipes up. "When you tell Gailen."

"Like what?"

Silence falls between us while we all think about it. Then we start talking. And plotting.

I had two hours to put it all together until Gailen came home.

Since we were together almost all the time, I never needed to leave him notes. It amused me and touched me when I learned that he kept every single one that I'd left him in the four years of him chasing my false trail.

I can hear him get home and move through the house. I can picture it perfectly.

The first note was on the front door.

Welcome home, G-money. Let's play a game.

The second was on the kitchen counter.

What did baby corn say to mama corn?

Where's pop corn?

The third is on the stairs.

What do you call a dad when he falls through the ice? A POPsicle!

"Aspen?" Gailen calls out for me, and I listen to him walk up the stairs and down the hall. The last note is sitting on our bed.

When does a dad joke become a dad joke? When it becomes apparent.

Underneath the paper with the joke is the positive test.

I open the door to the deck off our bedroom and lean against the door jamb.

Gailen turns to look at me, completely stunned.

"You're pregnant?"

"Yeah." I can't keep the grin off my face, and my stomach flutters when he grins back.

He rushes to me and picks me up, hugging me tight and burying his face in my neck. Gailen inhales me like he always does, and I hold onto him like I need him to live like I always do. The idea that all this love we have for each other is going to be shared with a little person we made is overwhelming and wonderful.

We pull back to keep smiling at each other.

"I never...this is beyond anything I thought I'd have in my life."

"Same," I laugh in response. "I didn't know I could dream like this until you."

I rest my forehead against his and squeeze him with my thighs.

"Love you," I whisper.

He whispers it back before kissing me.

Playlist

Natural - S Club 7

Better - the Vamps

Slow Hands - Niall Horan

Style - Taylor Swift

Ride It - Regard

You're Welcome - Dwayne Johnson, from *Moana*

Clarity - Zedd, Foxes

Ultralife - Oh Wonder

Acknowledgments

Husband. This one was so hard for me because I lost faith while writing it. Not in the story but in myself, and you took all of that in stride. This book would not exist without you, and this story was kind of fun and silly and exactly the end I needed to write. You're the best.

Thank you to Annie, Kim, Viktoriah, Jenn S, Jenn M, Brittany, my mom, my MIL, and the people who have read this series and messaged me about it, encouraged me to keep working on it, and been forgiving of the fact that I'm new to a lot of this and that it's going to be far from perfect. I keep going and get better because of the feedback and support of all of you.

Sophie Lark, you dream of a human. While I am so happy to say this series is officially my backlist and I can move on to other projects, I do not think I would have moved forward with anything without you. Thank you for being the voice that encouraged me, and just all around being a great person.

If you're still here, thank you.

Also by Ashley Mack

The Senses
The Sight of You (Alina and Derick)
The Taste of You (Aster and Freelancer)
The Sound of You (Aro and Harp)
The Feel of You (Anora and Owen)
The Scent of You (Aspen and Gailen)

Companion Novellas
Look at Me (Kade and Cara)
Savor Me (Dominic and Cleo)
Silence Me (Rebecca, Shane, and Connor)

Elmwood College Tales
Offerings (Colin and Elise)
Preservation (Rome and Cyn)
Transfigured (Tate and Halle)
Beguiled (Maeve and Bennett)
Constraint (Mathias and Willow)

About the Author

Ash lives in the Midwest with her husband, two girls, a dog, and a cat. She reads during every spare moment. She hopes that her characters go in new directions with terrifying, strong women who go feral for their men, and that sometimes the men are the damsels in distress who need saving. Connect on Instagram and Tiktok at @totalsassreads

You can connect with me on:

🌐 http://www.ashleymackauthor.com

Subscribe to my newsletter:

✉ http://www.ashleymackauthor.com/contact